THE ROMANCE OF

TRISTAN AND ISEULT

By J. Bedier

Translated by H. Belloc

CONTENTS

PART THE THIRD

PART THE FIRST

THE CHILDHOOD OF TRISTAN

My lords, if you would hear a high tale of love and of death, here is that of Tristan and Queen Iseult; how to their full joy, but to their sorrow also, they loved each other, and how at last they died of that love together upon one day; she by him and he by her.

Long ago, when Mark was King over Cornwall, Rivalen, King of Lyonesse, heard that Mark's enemies waged war on him; so he crossed the sea to bring him aid; and so faithfully did he serve him with counsel and sword that Mark gave him his sister Blanchefleur, whom King Rivalen loved most marvellously.

He wedded her in Tintagel Minster, but hardly was she wed when the news came to him that his old enemy Duke Morgan had fallen on Lyonesse and was wasting town and field. Then Rivalen manned his ships in haste, and took Blanchefleur with him to his far land; but she was with child. He landed below his castle of Kanoël and gave the Queen in ward to his Marshal Rohalt, and after that set off to wage his war.

Blanchefleur waited for him continually, but he did not come home, till she learnt upon a day that Duke Morgan had killed him in foul ambush. She did not weep: she made no cry or lamentation, but her limbs failed her and grew weak, and her soul was filled with a strong desire to be rid of the flesh, and though Rohalt tried to soothe her she would not hear. Three days she awaited re-union with her lord, and on the fourth she brought forth a son; and taking him in her arms she said:

"Little son, I have longed a while to see you, and now I see you the fairest thing ever a woman bore. In sadness came I hither, in sadness did I bring forth, and in sadness has your first feast day gone. And as by sadness you came into the world, your name shall be called Tristan; that is the child of sadness."

After she had said these words she kissed him, and immediately when she had kissed him she died.

Rohalt, the keeper of faith, took the child, but already Duke Morgan's men besieged the Castle of Kanoël all round about. There is a wise saying: "Fool-hardy was never hardy," and he was compelled to yield to Duke Morgan at his mercy: but for fear that Morgan might slay Rivalen's heir the Marshal hid him among his own sons.

When seven years were passed and the time had come to take the child from the women, Rohalt put Tristan under a good master, the Squire Gorvenal, and Gorvenal taught him in a few years the arts that go with barony. He taught him the use of lance and sword and 'scutcheon and bow, and how to cast stone quoits and to leap wide dykes also: and he taught him to hate every lie and felony and to keep his given word; and he taught him the various kinds of song and harp-playing, and the hunter's craft; and when the child rode among the young squires you would have said that he and his horse and his armour were all one thing. To see him so noble and so proud, broad in the shoulders, loyal, strong and right, all men glorified Rohalt in such a son. But Rohalt remembering Rivalen and Blanchefleur (of whose youth and grace all this was a resurrection) loved him indeed as a son, but in his heart revered him as his lord.

Now all his joy was snatched from him on a day when certain merchants of Norway, having lured Tristan to their ship, bore him off as a rich prize, though Tristan fought hard, as a young wolf struggles, caught in a gin. But it is a truth well proved, and every sailor knows it, that the sea will hardly bear a felon ship, and gives no aid to rapine. The sea rose and cast a dark storm round the ship and drove it eight days and eight nights at random, till the mariners caught through the mist a coast of awful cliffs and sea- ward rocks whereon the sea would have ground their hull to pieces: then they did penance, knowing that the anger of the sea came of the lad, whom they had stolen in an evil hour, and they vowed his deliverance and got ready a boat to put him, if it might be, ashore: then the wind, and sea fell and the sky shone, and as the Norway ship grew small in the offing, a quiet tide cast Tristan and the boat upon a beach of sand.

Painfully he climbed the cliff and saw, beyond, a lonely rolling heath and a forest stretching out and endless. And he wept, remembering Gorvenal, his father, and the land of Lyonesse. Then the distant cry of a hunt, with horse and hound, came suddenly and lifted his heart, and a tall stag broke cover at the forest edge. The pack and the hunt streamed after it with a tumult of cries and winding horns, but just as the hounds were racing clustered at the haunch, the quarry turned to bay at a stones throw from Tristan; a huntsman gave him the thrust, while all around the hunt had gathered and was winding the kill. But Tristan, seeing by the gesture of the huntsman that he made to cut the neck of the stag, cried out:

"My lord, what would you do? Is it fitting to cut up so noble a beast like any farm-yard hog? Is that the custom of this country?"

And the huntsman answered:

"Fair friend, what startles you? Why yes, first I take off the head of a stag, and then I cut it into four quarters and we carry it on our saddle bows to King Mark, our lord: So do we, and so since the days of the first huntsmen have done the Cornish men. If, however, you know of some nobler custom, teach it us: take this knife and we will learn it willingly."

Then Tristan kneeled and skinned the stag before he cut it up, and quartered it all in order leaving the crow-bone all whole, as is meet, and putting aside at the end the head, the haunch, the tongue and the great heart's vein; and the huntsmen and the kennel hinds stood over him with delight, and the Master Huntsman said:

"Friend, these are good ways. In what land learnt you them? Tell us your country and your name."

"Good lord, my name is Tristan, and I learnt these ways in my country of Lyonesse."

"Tristan," said the Master Huntsman, "God reward the father that brought you up so nobly; doubtless he is a baron, rich and strong."

Now Tristan knew both speech and silence, and he answered:

"No, lord; my father is a burgess. I left his home unbeknownst upon a ship that trafficked to a far place, for I wished to learn how men lived in foreign lands. But if you will accept me of the hunt I will follow you gladly and teach you other crafts of venery."

"Fair Tristan, I marvel there should be a land where a burgess's son can know what a knight's son knows not elsewhere, but come with us since you will it; and welcome: we will bring you to King Mark, our lord."

Tristan completed his task; to the dogs he gave the heart, the head, offal and ears; and he taught the hunt how the skinning and the ordering should be done. Then he thrust the pieces upon pikes and gave them to this huntsman and to that to carry, to one the snout to another the haunch to another the flank to another the chine; and he taught them how to ride by twos in rank, according to the dignity of the pieces each might bear.

So they took the road and spoke together, till they came on a great castle and round it fields and orchards, and living waters and fish ponds and plough lands, and many ships were in its haven, for that castle stood above the sea. It was well fenced against all assault or engines of war, and its keep, which the giants had built long ago, was compact of great stones, like a chess board of vert and azure.

And when Tristan asked its name:

"Good liege," they said, "we call it Tintagel."

And Tristan cried:

"Tintagel! Blessed be thou of God, and blessed be they that dwell within thee."

(Therein, my lords, therein had Rivalen taken Blanchefleur to wife, though their son knew it not.)

When they came before the keep the horns brought the barons to the gates and King Mark himself. And when the Master Huntsman had told him all the story, and King Mark had marvelled at the good order of the cavalcade, and the cutting of the stag, and the high art of venery in all, yet most he wondered at the stranger boy, and still gazed at him, troubled and wondering whence came his tenderness, and his heart would answer him nothing; but, my lords, it was blood that spoke, and the love he had long since borne his sister Blanchefleur.

That evening, when the boards were cleared, a singer out of Wales, a master, came forward among the barons in Hall and sang a harper's song, and as this harper touched the strings of his harp, Tristan who sat at the King's feet, spoke thus to him:

"Oh master, that is the first of songs! The Bretons of old wove it once to chant the loves of Graëlent. And the melody is rare and rare are the words: master, your voice is subtle: harp us that well."

But when the Welshman had sung, he answered:

"Boy, what do you know of the craft of music? If the burgesses of Lyonesse teach their sons harp—play also, and rotes and viols too, rise, and take this harp and show your skill."

Then Tristan took the harp and sang so well that the barons softened as they heard, and King Mark marvelled at the harper from Lyonesse whither so long ago Rivalen had taken Blanchefleur away.

When the song ended, the King was silent a long space, but he said at last:

"Son, blessed be the master that taught thee, and blessed be thou of God: for God loves good singers. Their voices and the voice of the harp enter the souls of men and wake dear memories and cause them to forget many a mourning and many a sin. For our joy did you come to this roof, stay near us a long time, friend."

And Tristan answered:

"Very willingly will I serve you, sire, as your harper, your huntsman and your liege."

So did he, and for three years a mutual love grew up in their hearts. By day Tristan followed King Mark at pleas and in saddle; by night he slept in the royal room with the councillors and the peers, and if the King was sad he would harp to him to soothe his care. The barons also cherished him, and (as you shall learn) Dinas of Lidan, the seneschal, beyond all others. And more tenderly than the barons and than Dinas the King loved him. But Tristan could not forget, or Rohalt his father, or his master Gorvenal, or the land of Lyonesse.

My lords, a teller that would please, should not stretch his tale too long, and truly this tale is so various and so high that it needs no straining. Then let me shortly tell how Rohalt himself, after long wandering by sea and land, came into Cornwall, and found Tristan, and showing the King the carbuncle that once was Blanchefleur's, said:

"King Mark, here is your nephew Tristan, son of your sister Blanchefleur and of King Rivalen. Duke Morgan holds his land most wrongfully; it is time such land came back to its lord."

And Tristan (in a word) when his uncle had armed him knight, crossed the sea, and was hailed of his father's vassals, and killed Rivalen's slayer and was re-seized of his land.

Then remembering how King Mark could no longer live in joy without him, he summoned his council and his barons and said this:

"Lords of the Lyonesse, I have retaken this place and I have avenged King Rivalen by the help of God and of you. But two men Rohalt and King Mark of Cornwall nourished me, an orphan, and a wandering boy. So should I call them also fathers. Now a free man has two things thoroughly his own, his body and his land. To Rohalt then, here, I will release my land. Do you hold it, father, and your son shall hold it after you. But my body I give up to King Mark. I will leave this country, dear though it be, and in Cornwall I will serve King Mark as my lord. Such is my judgment, but you, my lords of Lyonesse, are my lieges, and owe me counsel; if then, some one of you will counsel me another thing let him rise and speak."

But all the barons praised him, though they wept; and taking with him Gorvenal only, Tristan set sail for King Mark's land.

THE MORHOLT OUT OF IRELAND

When Tristan came back to that land, King Mark and all his Barony were mourning; for the King of Ireland had manned a fleet to ravage Cornwall, should King Mark refuse, as he had refused these fifteen years, to pay a tribute his fathers had paid. Now that year this King had sent to Tintagel, to carry his summons, a giant knight; the Morholt, whose sister he had wed, and whom no man had yet been able to overcome: so King Mark had summoned all the barons of his land to Council, by letters sealed.

On the day assigned, when the barons were gathered in hall, and when the King had taken his throne, the Morholt said these things:

"King Mark, hear for the last time the summons of the King of Ireland, my lord. He arraigns you to pay at last that which you have owed so long, and because you have refused it too long already he bids you give over to me this day three hundred youths and three hundred maidens drawn by lot from among the Cornish folk. But if so be that any would prove by trial of combat that the King of Ireland receives this tribute without right, I will take up his wager. Which among you, my Cornish lords, will fight to redeem this land?"

The barons glanced at each other but all were silent.

Then Tristan knelt at the feet of King Mark and said:

"Lord King, by your leave I will do battle."

And in vain would King Mark have turned him from his purpose, thinking, how could even valour save so young a knight? But he threw down his gage to the Morholt, and the Morholt took up the gage.

On the appointed day he had himself clad for a great feat of arms in a hauberk and in a steel helm, and he entered a boat and drew to the islet of St. Samson's, where the knights were to fight each to each alone. Now the Morholt had hoisted to his mast a sail of rich purple, and coming fast to land, he moored his boat on the shore. But Tristan pushed off his own boat adrift with his feet, and said:

"One of us only will go hence alive. One boat will serve."

And each rousing the other to the fray they passed into the isle.

No man saw the sharp combat; but thrice the salt sea-breeze had wafted or seemed to waft a cry of fury to the land, when at last towards the hour of noon the purple sail showed far off; the Irish boat appeared from the island shore, and there rose a clamour of "the Morholt!" When suddenly, as the boat grew larger on the sight and topped a wave, they saw that Tristan stood on the prow holding a sword in his hand. He leapt ashore, and as the mothers kissed the steel upon his feet he cried to the Morholt's men:

"My lords of Ireland, the Morholt fought well. See here, my sword is broken and a splinter of it stands fast in his head. Take you that steel, my lords; it is the tribute of Cornwall."

Then he went up to Tintagel and as he went the people he had freed waved green boughs, and rich cloths were hung at the windows. But when Tristan reached the castle with joy, songs and joy-bells sounding about him, he drooped in the arms of King Mark, for the blood ran from his wounds.

The Morholt's men, they landed in Ireland quite cast down. For when ever he came back into Whitehaven the Morholt had been wont to take joy in the sight of his clan upon the shore, of the Queen his sister, and of his niece Iseult the Fair. Tenderly had they cherished him of old, and had he taken some wound, they healed him, for they were skilled in balms and potions. But now their magic was vain, for he lay dead and the splinter of the foreign brand yet stood in his skull till Iseult plucked it out and shut it in a chest.

From that day Iseult the Fair knew and hated the name of Tristan of Lyonesse.

But over in Tintagel Tristan languished, for there trickled a poisonous blood from his wound. The doctors found that the Morholt had thrust into him a poisoned barb, and as their potions and their theriac could never heal him they left him in God's hands. So hateful a stench came from his wound that all his dearest friends fled him, all save King Mark, Gorvenal and Dinas of Lidan. They always could stay near his couch because their love overcame their abhorrence. At last Tristan had himself carried into a boat apart on the shore; and lying facing the sea he awaited death, for he thought: "I must die; but it is good to see the sun and my heart is still high. I would like to try the sea that brings all chances. ... I would have the sea bear me far off alone, to what land no matter, so that it heal me of my wound."

He begged so long that King Mark accepted his desire. He bore him into a boat with neither sail nor oar, and Tristan wished that his harp only should be placed beside him: for sails he could not lift, nor oar ply, nor sword wield; and as a seaman on some long voyage casts to the sea a beloved companion dead, so Gorvenal pushed out to sea that boat where his dear son lay; and the sea drew him away.

For seven days and seven nights the sea so drew him; at times to charm his grief, he harped; and when at last the sea brought him near a shore where fishermen had left their port that night to fish far out, they heard as they rowed a sweet and strong and living tune that ran above the sea, and feathering their oars they listened immovable.

In the first whiteness of the dawn they saw the boat at large: she went at random and nothing seemed to live in her except the voice of the harp. But as they neared, the air grew weaker and died; and when they hailed her Tristan's hands had fallen lifeless on the strings though they still trembled. The fishermen took him in and bore him back to port, to their lady who was merciful and perhaps would heal him.

It was that same port of Whitehaven where the Morholt lay, and their lady was Iseult the Fair.

She alone, being skilled in philtres, could save Tristan, but she alone wished him dead. When Tristan knew himself again (for her art restored him) he knew himself to be in the land of peril. But he was yet strong to hold his own and found good crafty words. He told a tale of how he was a seer that had taken passage on a merchant ship and sailed to Spain to learn the art of reading all the stars,—of how pirates had boarded the ship and of how, though wounded, he had fled into that boat. He was believed, nor did any of the Morholt's men know his face again, so hardly had the poison used it. But when, after forty days, Iseult of the Golden Hair had all but healed him, when already his limbs had recovered and the grace of youth returned, he knew that he must escape, and he fled and after many dangers he came again before Mark the King.

THE QUEST OF THE LADY WITH THE HAIR OF GOLD

My lords, there were in the court of King Mark four barons the basest of men, who hated Tristan with a hard hate, for his greatness and for the tender love the King bore him. And well I know their names: Andret, Guenelon, Gondoïne and Denoalen. They knew that the King had intent to grow old childless and to leave his land to Tristan; and their envy swelled and by lies they angered the chief men of Cornwall against Tristan. They said:

"There have been too many marvels in this man's life. It was marvel enough that he beat the Morholt, but by what sorcery did he try the sea alone at the point of death, or which of us, my lords, could voyage without mast or sail? They say that warlocks can. It was sure a warlock feat, and that is a warlock harp of his pours poison daily into the King's heart. See how he has bent that heart by power and chain of sorcery! He will be king yet, my lords, and you will hold your lands of a wizard."

They brought over the greater part of the barons and these pressed King Mark to take to wife some king's daughter who should give him an heir, or else they threatened to return each man into his keep and wage him war. But the King turned against them and swore in his heart that so long as his dear nephew lived no king's daughter should come to his bed. Then in his turn did Tristan (in his shame to be thought to serve for hire) threaten that if the King did not yield to his barons, he would himself go over sea serve some great king. At this, King Mark made a term with his barons and gave them forty days to hear his decision.

On the appointed day he waited alone in his chamber and sadly mused: "Where shall I find a king's daughter so fair and yet so distant that I may feign to wish her my wife?"

13

Just then by his window that looked upon the sea two building swallows came in quarrelling together. Then, startled, they flew out, but had let fall from their beaks a woman's hair, long and fine, and shining like a beam of light.

King Mark took it, and called his barons and Tristan and said:

"To please you, lords, I will take a wife; but you must seek her whom I have chosen."

"Fair lord, we wish it all," they said, "and who may she be?"

"Why," said he, "she whose hair this is; nor will I take another."

"And whence, lord King, comes this Hair of Gold; who brought it and from what land?"

"It comes, my lords, from the Lady with the Hair of Gold, the swallows brought it me. They know from what country it came."

Then the barons saw themselves mocked and cheated, and they turned with sneers to Tristan, for they thought him to have counselled the trick. But Tristan, when he had looked on the Hair of Gold, remembered Iseult the Fair and smiled and said this:

"King Mark, can you not see that the doubts of these lords shame me? You have designed in vain. I will go seek the Lady with the Hair of Gold. The search is perilous: never the less, my uncle, I would once more put my body and my life into peril for you; and that your barons may know I love you loyally, I take this oath, to die on the adventure or to bring back to this castle of Tintagel the Queen with that fair hair."

He fitted out a great ship and loaded it with corn and wine, with honey and all manner of good things; he manned it with Gorvenal and a hundred young knights of high birth, chosen among the bravest, and he clothed them in coats of home-spun and in hair cloth so that they seemed merchants only: but under the deck he hid rich cloth of gold and scarlet as for a great king's messengers.

When the ship had taken the sea the helmsman asked him:

"Lord, to what land shall I steer?"

"Sir," said he, "steer for Ireland, straight for Whitehaven harbour."

At first Tristan made believe to the men of Whitehaven that his friends were merchants of England come peacefully to barter; but as these strange merchants passed the day in the useless games of draughts and chess, and seemed to know dice better than the bargain price of corn, Tristan feared discovery and knew not how to pursue his quest.

Now it chanced once upon the break of day that he heard a cry so terrible that one would have called it a demon's cry; nor had he ever heard a brute bellow in such wise, so awful and strange it seemed. He called a woman who passed by the harbour, and said:

"Tell me, lady, whence comes that voice I have heard, and hide me nothing."

"My lord," said she, "I will tell you truly. It is the roar of a dragon the most terrible and dauntless upon earth. Daily it leaves its den and stands at one of the gates of the city: Nor can any come out or go in till a maiden has been given up to it; and when it has her in its claws it devours her."

"Lady," said Tristan, "make no mock of me, but tell me straight: Can a man born of woman kill this thing?"

"Fair sir, and gentle," she said, "I cannot say; but this is sure: Twenty knights and tried have run the venture, because the King of Ireland has published it that he will give his daughter, Iseult the Fair, to whomsoever shall kill the beast; but it has devoured them all."

Tristan left the woman and returning to his ship armed himself in secret, and it was a fine sight to see so noble a charger and so good a knight come out from such a merchant-hull: but the haven was empty of folk, for the dawn had barely broken and none saw him as he rode to the gate. And hardly had he passed it, when he met suddenly five men at full gallop flying towards the town. Tristan seized one by his hair, as he passed, and dragged him over his mount's crupper and held him fast:

"God save you, my lord," said he, "and whence does the dragon come?" And when the other had shown him by what road, he let him go.

As the monster neared, he showed the head of a bear and red eyes like coals of fire and hairy tufted ears; lion's claws, a serpent's tail, and a griffin's body.

Tristan charged his horse at him so strongly that, though the beast's mane stood with fright yet he drove at the dragon: his lance struck its scales and shivered. Then Tristan drew his sword and struck at the dragon's head, but he did not so much as cut the hide. The beast felt the blow: with its claws he dragged at the shield and broke it from the arm; then, his breast unshielded, Tristan used the sword again and struck so strongly that the air rang all round about: but in vain, for he could not wound and meanwhile the dragon vomited from his nostrils two streams of loath-some flames, and Tristan's helm blackened like a cinder and his horse stumbled and fell down and died; but Tristan standing on his feet thrust his sword right into the beast's jaws, and split its heart in two.

Then he cut out the tongue and put it into his hose, but as the poison came against his flesh the hero fainted and fell in the high grass that bordered the marsh around.

Now the man he had stopped in flight was the Seneschal of Ireland and he desired Iseult the Fair: and though he was a coward, he had dared so far as to return with his companions secretly, and he found the dragon dead; so he cut off its head and bore it to the King, and claimed the great reward.

The King could credit his prowess but hardly, yet wished justice done and summoned his vassals to court, so that there, before the Barony assembled, the seneschal should furnish proof of his victory won.

When Iseult the Fair heard that she was to be given to this coward first she laughed long, and then she wailed. But on the morrow, doubting some trick, she took with her Perinis her squire and Brangien her maid, and all three rode unbeknownst towards the dragon's lair: and Iseult saw such a trail on the road as made her wonder—for the hoofs that made it had never been shod in her land. Then she came on the dragon, headless, and a dead horse beside him: nor was the horse harnessed in the fashion of Ireland. Some foreign man had slain the beast, but they knew not whether he still lived or no.

They sought him long, Iseult and Perinis and Brangien together, till at last Brangien saw the helm glittering in the marshy grass: and Tristan still breathed. Perinis put him on his horse and bore him secretly to the women's rooms. There Iseult told her mother the tale and left the hero with her, and as the Queen unharnessed him, the dragon's tongue fell from his boot of steel. Then, the Queen of Ireland revived him by the virtue of an herb and said:

"Stranger, I know you for the true slayer of the dragon: but our seneschal, a felon, cut off its head and claims my daughter Iseult for his wage; will you be ready two days hence to give him the lie in battle?"

"Queen," said he, "the time is short, but you, I think, can cure me in two days. Upon the dragon I conquered Iseult, and on the seneschal perhaps I shall reconquer her."

Then the Queen brewed him strong brews, and on the morrow Iseult the Fair got him ready a bath and anointed him with a balm her mother had conjured, and as he looked at her he thought, "So I have found the Queen of the Hair of Gold," and he smiled as he thought it. But Iseult, noting it, thought, "Why does he smile, or what have I neglected of the things due to a guest? He smiles to think I have for— gotten to burnish his armour."

She went and drew the sword from its rich sheath, but when she saw the splinter gone and the gap in the edge she thought of the Morholt's head. She balanced a moment in doubt, then she went to where she kept the steel she had found in the skull and she put it to the sword, and it fitted so that the join was hardly seen.

She ran to where Tristan lay wounded, and with the sword above him she cried:

"You are that Tristan of the Lyonesse, who killed the Morholt, my mother's brother, and now you shall die in your turn."

Tristan strained to ward the blow, but he was too weak; his wit, however, stood firm in spite of evil and he said:

"So be it, let me die: but to save yourself long memories, listen awhile. King's daughter, my life is not only in your power but is yours of right. My life is yours because you have twice returned it me. Once, long ago: for I was the wounded harper whom you healed of the poison of the Morholt's shaft. Nor repent the healing: were not these wounds had in fair fight? Did I kill the Morholt by treason? Had he not defied me and was I not held to the defence of my body? And now this second time also you have saved me. It was for you I fought the beast.

"But let us leave these things. I would but show you how my life is your own. Then if you kill me of right for the glory of it, you may ponder for long years, praising yourself that you killed a wounded guest who had wagered his life in your gaining."

Iseult replied: "I hear strange words. Why should he that killed the Morholt seek me also, his niece? Doubtless because the Morholt came for a tribute of maidens from Cornwall, so you came to boast returning that you had brought back the maiden who was nearest to him, to Cornwall, a slave."

"King's daughter," said Tristan, "No. ... One day two swallows flew, and flew to Tintagel and bore one hair out of all your hairs of gold, and I thought they brought me good will and peace, so I came to find you over-seas. See here, amid the threads of gold upon my coat your hair is sown: the threads are tarnished, but your bright hair still shines."

Iseult put down the sword and taking up the Coat of Arms she saw upon it the Hair of Gold and was silent a long space, till she kissed him on the lips to prove peace, and she put rich garments over him.

On the day of the barons' assembly, Tristan sent Perinis privily to his ship to summon his companions that they should come to court adorned as befitted the envoys of a great king.

One by one the hundred knights passed into the hall where all the barons of Ireland stood, they entered in silence and sat all in rank together: on their scarlet and purple the gems gleamed.

When the King had taken his throne, the seneschal arose to prove by witness and by arms that he had slain the dragon and that so Iseult was won. Then Iseult bowed to her father and said:

"King, I have here a man who challenges your seneschal for lies and felony. Promise that you will pardon this man all his past deeds, who stands to prove that he and none other slew the dragon, and grant him forgiveness and your peace."

The King said, "I grant it." But Iseult said, "Father, first give me the kiss of peace and forgiveness, as a sign that you will give him the same."

Then she found Tristan and led him before the Barony. And as he came the hundred knights rose all together, and crossed their arms upon their breasts and bowed, so the Irish knew that he was their lord.

But among the Irish many knew him again and cried, "Tristan of Lyonesse that slew the Morholt!" They drew their swords and clamoured for death. But Iseult cried: "King, kiss this man upon the lips as your oath was," and the King kissed him, and the clamour fell.

Then Tristan showed the dragon's tongue and offered the seneschal battle, but the seneschal looked at his face and dared not.

Then Tristan said: "My lords, you have said it, and it is truth: I killed the Morholt. But I crossed the sea to offer you a good blood-fine, to ransom that deed and get me quit of it. I put my body in peril of death and rid you of the beast and have so conquered Iseult the Fair, and having conquered her I will bear her away on my ship.

"But that these lands of Cornwall and Ireland may know no more hatred, but love only, learn that King Mark, my lord, will marry her. Here stand a hundred knights of high name, who all will swear with an oath upon the relics of the holy saints, that King Mark sends you by their embassy offer of peace and of brotherhood and goodwill; and that he would by your courtesy hold Iseult as his honoured wife, and that he would have all the men of Cornwall serve her as their Queen." When the lords of Ireland heard this they acclaimed it, and the King also was content.

Then, since that treaty and alliance was to be made, the King her father took Iseult by the hand and asked of Tristan that he should take an oath; to wit that he would lead her loyally to his lord, and Tristan took that oath and swore it before the knights and the Barony of Ireland assembled. Then the King put Iseult's right hand into Tristan's right hand, and Tristan held it for a space in token of seizin for the King of Cornwall. So, for the love of King Mark, did Tristan conquer the Queen of the Hair of Gold.

THE PHILTRE

When the day of Iseult's livery to the Lords of Cornwall drew near, her mother gathered herbs and flowers and roots and steeped them in wine, and brewed a potion of might, and having done so, said apart to Brangien:

"Child, it is yours to go with Iseult to King Mark's country, for you love her with a faithful love. Take then this pitcher and remember well my words. Hide it so that no eye shall see nor no lip go near it: but when the wedding night has come and that moment in which the wedded are left alone, pour this essenced wine into a cup and offer it to King Mark and to Iseult his queen. Oh! Take all care, my child, that they alone shall taste this brew. For this is its power: they who drink of it together love each other with their every single sense and with their every thought, forever, in life and in death."

And Brangien promised the Queen that she would do her bidding.

On the bark that bore her to Tintagel Iseult the Fair was weeping as she remembered her own land, and mourning swelled her heart, and she said, "Who am I that I should leave you to follow unknown men, my mother and my land? Accursed be the sea that bears me, for rather would I lie dead on the earth where I was born than live out there, beyond. ...

One day when the wind had fallen and the sails hung slack Tristan dropped anchor by an Island and the hundred knights of Cornwall and the sailors, weary of the sea, landed all. Iseult alone remained aboard and a little serving maid, when Tristan came near the Queen to calm her sorrow. The sun was hot above them and they were athirst and, as they called, the little maid looked about for drink for them and found that pitcher which the mother of Iseult had given into Brangien's keeping. And when she came on it, the child cried, "I have found you wine!" Now she had found not wine — but Passion and Joy most sharp, and Anguish without end, and Death.

The Queen drank deep of that draught and gave it to Tristan and he drank also long and emptied it all.

Brangien came in upon them; she saw them gazing at each other in silence as though ravished and apart; she saw before them the pitcher standing there; she snatched it up and cast it into the shuddering sea and cried aloud: "Cursed be the day I was born and cursed the day that first I trod this deck. Iseult, my friend, and Tristan, you, you have drunk death together."

And once more the bark ran free for Tintagel. But it seemed to Tristan as though an ardent briar, sharp-thorned but with flower most sweet smelling, drave roots into his blood and laced the lovely body of Iseult all round about it and bound it to his own and to his every thought and desire. And he thought, "Felons, that charged me with coveting King Mark's land, I have come lower by far, for it is not his land I covet. Fair uncle, who loved me orphaned ere ever you knew in me the blood of your sister Blanchefleur, you that wept as you bore me to that boat alone, why did you not drive out the boy that was to betray you? Ah! What thought was that! Iseult is yours and I am but your vassal; Iseult is yours and I am your son; Iseult is yours and may not love me."

But Iseult loved him, though she would have hated. She could not hate, for a tenderness more sharp than hatred tore her.

And Brangien watched them in anguish, suffering more cruelly because she alone knew the depth of evil done.

Two days she watched them, seeing them refuse all food or comfort and seeking each other as blind men seek, wretched apart and together more wretched still, for then they trembled each for the first avowal.

On the third day, as Tristan neared the tent on deck where Iseult sat, she saw him coming and she said to him, very humbly, "Come in, my lord."

"Queen," said Tristan, "why do you call me lord? Am I not your liege and vassal, to revere and serve and cherish you as my lady and Queen?"

But Iseult answered, "No, you know that you are my lord and my master, and I your slave. Ah, why did I not sharpen those wounds of the wounded singer, or let die that dragon-slayer in the grasses of the marsh? But then I did not know what now I know!"

"And what is it that you know, Iseult?"

She laid her arm upon Tristan's shoulder, the light of her eyes was drowned and her lips trembled.

"The love of you," she said. Whereat he put his lips to hers.

But as they thus tasted their first joy, Brangien, that watched them, stretched her arms and cried at their feet in tears:

"Stay and return if still you can ... But oh! that path has no returning. For already Love and his strength drag you on and now henceforth forever never shall you know joy without pain again. The wine possesses you, the draught your mother gave me, the draught the King alone should have drunk with you: but that old Enemy has tricked us, all us three; friend Tristan, Iseult my friend, for that bad ward I kept take here my body and my life, for through me and in that cup you have drunk not love alone, but love and death together."

The lovers held each other; life and desire trembled through their youth, and Tristan said, "Well then, come Death."

And as evening fell, upon the bark that heeled and ran to King Mark's land, they gave themselves up utterly to love.

THE TALL PINE-TREE

As King Mark came down to greet Iseult upon the shore, Tristan took her hand and led her to the King and the King took seizin of her, taking her hand. He led her in great pomp to his castle of Tintagel, and as she came in hall amid the vassals her beauty shone so that the walls were lit as they are lit at dawn. Then King Mark blessed those swallows which, by happy courtesy, had brought the Hair of Gold, and Tristan also he blessed, and the hundred knights who, on that adventurous bark, had gone to find him joy of heart and of eyes; yet to him also that ship was to bring sting, torment and mourning.

And on the eighteenth day, having called his Barony together he took Iseult to wife. But on the wedding night, to save her friend, Brangien took her place in the darkness, for her remorse demanded even this from her; nor was the trick discovered.

Then Iseult lived as a queen, but lived in sadness. She had King Mark's tenderness and the barons' honour; the people also loved her; she passed her days amid the frescoes on the walls and floors all strewn with flowers; good jewels had she and purple cloth and tapestry of Hungary and Thessaly too, and songs of harpers, and curtains upon which were worked leopards and eagles and popinjays and all the beasts of sea and field. And her love too she had, love high and splendid, for as is the custom among great lords, Tristan could ever be near her. At his leisure and his dalliance, night and day: for he slept in the King's chamber as great lords do, among the lieges and the councillors. Yet still she feared; for though her love were secret and Tristan unsuspected (for who suspects a son?) Brangien knew. And Brangien seemed in the Queen's mind like a witness spying; for Brangien alone knew what manner of life she led, and held her at mercy so. And the Queen thought Ah, if some day she should weary of serving as a slave the bed where once she passed for Queen ... If Tristan should die from her betrayal! So fear

25

maddened the Queen, but not in truth the fear of Brangien who was loyal; her own heart bred the fear.

Not Brangien who was faithful, not Brangien, but themselves had these lovers to fear, for hearts so stricken will lose their vigilance. Love pressed them hard, as thirst presses the dying stag to the stream; love dropped upon them from high heaven, as a hawk slipped after long hunger falls right upon the bird. And love will not be hidden. Brangien indeed by her prudence saved them well, nor ever were the Queen and her lover unguarded. But in every hour and place every man could see Love terrible, that rode them, and could see in these lovers their every sense overflowing like new wine working in the vat.

The four felons at court who had hated Tristan of old for his prowess, watched the Queen; they had guessed that great love, and they burnt with envy and hatred and now a kind of evil joy. They planned to give news of their watching to the King, to see his tenderness turned to fury, Tristan thrust out or slain, and the Queen in torment; for though they feared Tristan their hatred mastered their fear; and, on a day, the four barons called King Mark to parley, and Andret said:

"Fair King, your heart will be troubled and we four also mourn; yet are we bound to tell you what we know. You have placed your trust in Tristan and Tristan would shame you. In vain we warned you. For the love of one man you have mocked ties of blood and all your Barony. Learn then that Tristan loves the Queen; it is truth proved and many a word is passing on it now."

The royal King shrank and answered:

"Coward! What thought was that? Indeed I have placed my trust in Tristan. And rightly, for on the day when the Morholt offered combat to you all, you hung your heads and were dumb, and you trembled before him; but Tristan dared him for the honour of this land, and took mortal wounds. Therefore do you hate him, and therefore do I cherish him beyond thee, Andret, and beyond any other; but what then have you seen or heard or known?"

"Naught, lord, save what your eyes could see or your ears hear. Look you and listen, Sire, if there is yet time."

And they left him to taste the poison.

Then King Mark watched the Queen and Tristan; but Brangien noting it warned them both and the King watched in vain, so that, soon wearying of an ignoble task, but knowing (alas!) that he could not kill his uneasy thought, he sent for Tristan and said:

"Tristan, leave this castle; and having left it, remain apart and do not think to return to it, and do not repass its moat or boundaries. Felons have charged you with an awful treason, but ask me nothing; I could not speak their words without shame to us both, and for your part seek you no word to appease. I have not believed them ... had I done so ... But their evil words have troubled all my soul and only by your absence can my disquiet be soothed. Go, doubtless I will soon recall you. Go, my son, you are still dear to me.

When the felons heard the news they said among themselves, "He is gone, the wizard; he is driven out. Surely he will cross the sea on far adventures to carry his traitor service to some distant King."

But Tristan had not strength to depart altogether; and when he had crossed the moats and boundaries of the Castle he knew he could go no further. He stayed in Tintagel town and lodged with Gorvenal in a burgess' house, and languished oh! more wounded than when in that past day the shaft of the Morholt had tainted his body.

In the close towers Iseult the Fair drooped also, but more wretched still. For it was hers all day long to feign laughter and all night long to conquer fever and despair. And all night as she lay by King Mark's side, fever still kept her waking, and she stared at darkness. She longed to fly to Tristan and she dreamt dreams of running to the gates and of finding there sharp scythes, traps of the felons, that cut her tender knees; and she dreamt of weakness and falling, and that her wounds had left her blood upon the ground. Now these lovers would have died, but Brangien succoured them. At peril of her life she found the house where Tristan lay. There Gorvenal opened to her very gladly, knowing what salvation she could bring.

So she found Tristan, and to save the lovers she taught him a device, nor was ever known a more subtle ruse of love.

Behind the castle of Tintagel was an orchard fenced around and wide and all closed in with stout and pointed stakes and numberless trees were there and fruit on them, birds and clusters of sweet grapes. And furthest from the castle, by the stakes of the pallisade, was a tall pine-tree, straight and with heavy branches spreading from its trunk. At its root a living spring welled calm into a marble round, then ran between two borders winding, throughout the orchard and so, on, till it flowed at last within the castle and through the women's rooms.

And every evening, by Brangien's counsel, Tristan cut him twigs and bark, leapt the sharp stakes and, having come beneath the pine, threw them into the clear spring; they floated light as foam down the stream to the women's rooms; and Iseult watched for their coming, and on those evenings she would wander out into the orchard and find her friend. Lithe and in fear would she come, watching at every step for what might lurk in the trees observing, foes or the felons whom she knew, till she spied Tristan; and the night and the branches of the pine protected them.

And so she said one night: "Oh, Tristan, I have heard that the castle is faëry and that twice a year it vanishes away. So is it vanished now and this is that enchanted orchard of which the harpers sing." And as she said it, the sentinels bugled dawn.

Iseult had refound her joy. Mark's thought of ill-ease grew faint; but the felons felt or knew which way lay truth, and they guessed that Tristan had met the Queen. Till at last Duke Andret (whom God shame) said to his peers:

"My lords, let us take counsel of Frocin the Dwarf; for he knows the seven arts, and magic and every kind of charm. He will teach us if he will the wiles of Iseult the Fair."

The little evil man drew signs for them and characters of sorcery; he cast the fortunes of the hour and then at last he said:

"Sirs, high good lords, this night shall you seize them both."

Then they led the little wizard to the King, and he said:

"Sire, bid your huntsmen leash the hounds and saddle the horses, proclaim a seven days' hunt in the forest and seven nights abroad therein, and hang me high if you do not hear this night what converse Tristan holds."

So did the King unwillingly; and at fall of night he left the hunt taking the dwarf in pillion, and entered the orchard, and the dwarf took him to the tall pine-tree, saying:

"Fair King, climb into these branches and take with you your arrows and your bow, for you may need them; and bide you still."

That night the moon shone clear. Hid in the branches the King saw his nephew leap the pallisades and throw his bark and twigs into the stream. But Tristan had bent over the round well to throw them and so doing had seen the image of the King. He could not stop the branches as they floated away, and there, yonder, in the women's rooms, Iseult was watching and would come.

She came, and Tristan watched her motionless. Above him in the tree he heard the click of the arrow when it fits the string.

She came, but with more prudence than her wont, thinking, "What has passed, that Tristan does not come to meet me? He has seen some foe."

29

Suddenly, by the clear moonshine, she also saw the King's shadow in the fount. She showed the wit of women well, she did not lift her eyes.

"Lord God," she said, low down, grant I may be the first to speak."

"Tristan," she said, "what have you dared to do, calling me hither at such an hour? Often have you called me —to beseech, you said. And Queen though I am, I know you won me that title—and I have come. What would you?"

"Queen, I would have you pray the King for me."

She was in tears and trembling, but Tristan praised God the Lord who had shown his friend her peril.

"Queen," he went on, "often and in vain have I summoned you; never would you come. Take pity; the King hates me and I know not why. Perhaps you know the cause and can charm his anger. For whom can he trust if not you, chaste Queen and courteous, Iseult?"

"Truly, Lord Tristan, you do not know he doubts us both. And I, to add to my shame, must acquaint you of it. Ah! but God knows if I lie, never went cut my love to any man but he that first received me. And would you have me, at such a time, implore your pardon of the King? Why, did he know of my passage here to-night he would cast my ashes to the wind. My body trembles and I am afraid. I go, for I have waited too long."

In the branches the King smiled and had pity.

And as Iseult fled: "Queen," said Tristan, "in the Lord's name help me, for charity."

"Friend," she replied, "God aid you! The King wrongs you but the Lord God will be by you in whatever land you go."

So she went back to the women's rooms and told it to Brangien, who cried: "Iseult, God has worked a miracle for you, for He is compassionate and will not hurt the innocent in heart."

And when he had left the orchard, the King said smiling:

"Fair nephew, that ride you planned is over now."

But in an open glade apart, Frocin, the Dwarf, read in the clear stars that the King now meant his death; he blackened with shame and fear and fled into Wales.

THE DISCOVERY

King Mark made peace with Tristan. Tristan returned to the castle as of old. Tristan slept in the King's chamber with his peers. He could come or go, the King thought no more of it.

Mark had pardoned the felons, and as the seneschal, Dinas of Lidan, found the dwarf wandering in a forest abandoned, he brought him home, and the King had pity and pardoned even him.

But his goodness did but feed the ire of the barons, who swore this oath: If the King kept Tristan in the land they would withdraw to their strongholds as for war, and they called the King to parley.

"Lord," said they, "Drive you Tristan forth. He loves the Queen as all who choose can see, but as for us we will bear it no longer."

And the King sighed, looking down in silence.

" King," they went on, "we will not bear it, for we know now that this is known to you and that yet you will not move. Parley you, and take counsel. As for us if you will not exile this man, your nephew, and drive him forth out of your land forever, we will withdraw within our Bailiwicks and take our neighbours also from your court: for we cannot endure his presence longer in this place. Such is your balance: choose."

"My lords," said he, "once I hearkened to the evil words you spoke of Tristan, yet was I wrong in the end. But you are my lieges and I would not lose the service of my men. Counsel me therefore, I charge you, you that owe me counsel. You know me for a man neither proud nor overstepping."

"Lord," said they, "call then Frocin hither. You mistrust him for that orchard night. Still, was it not he that read in the stars of the Queen's coming there and to the very pine-tree too? He is very wise, take counsel of him."

And he came, did that hunchback of Hell: the felons greeted him and he planned this evil.

"Sire," said he, "let your nephew ride hard to-morrow at dawn with a brief drawn up on parchment and well sealed with a seal: bid him ride to King Arthur at Carduel. Sire, he sleeps with the peers in your chamber; go you out when the first sleep falls on men, and if he love Iseult so madly, why, then I swear by God and by the laws of Rome, he will try to speak with her before he rides. But if he do so unknown to you or to me, then slay me. As for the trap, let me lay it, but do you say nothing of his ride to him until the time for sleep."

And when King Mark had agreed, this dwarf did a vile thing. He bought of a baker four farthings' worth of flour, and hid it in the turn of his coat. That night, when the King had supped and the men-at-arms lay down to sleep in hall, Tristan came to the King as custom was, and the King said:

"Fair nephew, do my will: ride to-morrow night to King Arthur at Carduel, and give him this brief, with my greeting, that he may open it: and stay you with him but one day."

And when Tristan said: "I will take it on the morrow;"

The King added: "Aye, and before day dawn."

But, as the peers slept all round the King their lord, that night, a mad thought took Tristan that, before he rode, he knew not for how long, before dawn he would say a last word to the Queen. And there was a spear length in the darkness between them. Now the dwarf slept with the rest in the King's chamber, and when he thought that all slept he rose and scattered the flour silently in the spear length that lay between Tristan and the Queen; but Tristan watched and saw him, and said to himself:

"It is to mark my footsteps, but there shall be no marks to show."

At midnight, when all was dark in the room, no candle nor any lamp glimmering, the King went out silently by the door and with him the dwarf. Then Tristan rose in the darkness and judged the spear length and leapt the space between, for his farewell. But that day in the hunt a boar had wounded him in the leg, and in this effort the wound bled. He did not feel it or see it in the darkness, but the blood dripped upon the couches and the flour strewn between; and outside in the moonlight the dwarf read the heavens and knew what had been done and he cried:

"Enter, my King, and if you do not hold them, hang me high."

Then the King and the dwarf and the four felons ran in with lights and noise, and though Tristan had regained his place there was the blood for witness, and though Iseult feigned sleep, and Perinis too, who lay at Tristan's feet, yet there was the blood for witness. And the King looked in silence at the blood where it lay upon the bed and the boards and trampled into the flour.

And the four barons held Tristan down upon his bed and mocked the Queen also, promising her full justice; and they bared and showed the wound whence the blood flowed.

Then the King said:

"Tristan, now nothing longer holds. To-morrow you shall die."

And Tristan answered:

"Have mercy, Lord, in the name of God that suffered the Cross!"

But the felons called on the King to take vengeance, saying:

"Do justice, King: take vengeance."

And Tristan went on, "Have mercy, not on me—for why should I stand at dying?—Truly, but for you, I would have sold my honour high to cowards who, under your peace, have put hands on my

35

body—but in homage to you I have yielded and you may do with me what you will. But, lord, remember the Queen!"

And as he knelt at the King's feet he still complained:

"Remember the Queen; for if any man of your household make so bold as to maintain the lie that I loved her unlawfully I will stand up armed to him in a ring. Sire, in the name of God the Lord, have mercy on her."

Then the barons bound him with ropes, and the Queen also. But had Tristan known that trial by combat was to be denied him, certainly he would not have suffered it.

For he trusted in God and knew no man dared draw sword against him in the lists. And truly he did well to trust in God, for though the felons mocked him when he said he had loved loyally, yet I call you to witness, my lords who read this, and who know of the philtre drunk upon the high seas, and who, understand whether his love were disloyalty indeed. For men see this and that outward thing, but God alone the heart, and in the heart alone is crime and the sole final judge is God. Therefore did He lay down the law that a man accused might uphold his cause by battle, and God himself fights for the innocent in such a combat.

Therefore did Tristan claim justice and the right of battle and therefore was he careful to fail in nothing of the homage he owed King Mark, his lord.

But had he known what was coming, he would have killed the felons.

THE CHANTRY LEAP

Dark was the night, and the news ran that Tristan and the Queen were held and that the King would kill them; and wealthy burgess, or common man, they wept and ran to the palace.

And the murmurs and the cries ran through the city, but such was the King's anger in his castle above that not the strongest nor the proudest baron dared move him.

Night ended and the day drew near. Mark, before dawn, rode out to the place where he held pleas and judgment. He ordered a ditch to be dug in the earth and knotty vine-shoots and thorns to be laid therein.

At the hour of Prime he had a ban cried through his land to gather the men of Cornwall; they came with a great noise and the King spoke them thus:

"My lords, I have made here a faggot of thorns for Tristan and the Queen; for they have fallen."

But they cried all, with tears:

"A sentence, lord, a sentence; an indictment and pleas; for killing without trial is shame and crime."

But Mark answered in his anger:

"Neither respite, nor delay, nor pleas, nor sentence. By God that made the world, if any dare petition me, he shall burn first!"

He ordered the fire to be lit, and Tristan to be called.

The flames rose, and all were silent before the flames, and the King waited.

The servants ran to the room where watch was kept on the two lovers; and they dragged Tristan out by his hands though he wept for his honour; but as they dragged him off in such a shame, the Queen still called to him:

"Friend, if I die that you may live, that will be great joy."

Now, hear how full of pity is God and how He heard the lament and the prayers of the common folk, that day.

For as Tristan and his guards went down from the town to where the faggot burned, near the road upon a rock was a chantry, it stood at a cliff's edge steep and sheer, and it turned to the sea-breeze; in the apse of it were windows glazed. Then Tristan said to those with him:

"My lords, let me enter this chantry, to pray for a moment the mercy of God whom I have offended; my death is near. There is but one door to the place, my lords, and each of you has his sword drawn. So, you may well see that, when my prayer to God is done, I must come past you again: when I have prayed God, my lords, for the last time.

And one of the guards said: "Why, let him go in."

So they let him enter to pray. But he, once in, dashed through and leapt the altar rail and the altar too and forced a window of the apse, and leapt again over the cliff's edge. So might he die, but not of that shameful death before the people.

Now learn, my lords, how generous was God to him that day. The wind took Tristan's cloak and he fell upon a smooth rock at the cliff's foot, which to this day the men of Cornwall call "Tristan's leap."

His guards still waited for him at the chantry door, but vainly, for God was now his guard. And he ran, and the fine sand crunched under his feet, and far off he saw the faggot burning, and the smoke and the crackling flames; and fled.

Sword girt and bridle loose, Gorvenal had fled the city, lest the King burn him in his master's place: and he found Tristan on the shore.

"Master," said Tristan, "God has saved me, but oh! master, to what end? For without Iseult I may not and I will not live, and I rather had died of my fall. They will burn her for me, then I too will die for her."

"Lord," said Gorvenal, "take no counsel of anger. See here this thicket with a ditch dug round about it. Let us hide therein where the track passes near, and comers by it will tell us news; and, boy, if they burn Iseult, I swear by God, the Son of Mary, never to sleep under a roof again until she be avenged."

There was a poor man of the common folk that had seen Tristan's fall, and had seen him stumble and rise after, and he crept to Tintagel and to Iseult where she was bound, and said:

"Queen, weep no more. Your friend has fled safely."

"Then I thank God," said she, "and whether they bind or loose me, and whether they kill or spare me, I care but little now."

And though blood came at the cord-knots, so tightly had the traitors bound her, yet still she said, smiling:

"Did I weep for that when God has loosed my friend I should be little worth."

When the news came to the King that Tristan had leapt that leap and was lost he paled with anger, and bade his men bring forth Iseult.

They dragged her from the room, and she came before the crowd, held by her delicate hands, from which blood dropped, and the crowd called:

"Have pity on her—the loyal Queen and honoured! Surely they that gave her up brought mourning on us all—our curses on them!"

But the King's men dragged her to the thorn faggot as it blazed. She stood up before the flame, and the crowd cried its anger, and cursed the traitors and the King. None could see her without pity, unless he had a felon's heart: she was so tightly bound. The tears ran down her face and fell upon her grey gown where ran a little thread of gold, and a thread of gold was twined into her hair.

Just then there had come up a hundred lepers of the King's, deformed and broken, white horribly, and limping on their crutches. And they drew near the flame, and being evil, loved the sight. And their chief Ivan, the ugliest of them all, cried to the King in a quavering voice:

"O King, you would burn this woman in that flame, and it is sound justice, but too swift, for very soon the fire will fall, and her ashes will very soon be scattered by the high wind and her agony be done. Throw her rather to your lepers where she may drag out a life for ever asking death."

And the King answered:

"Yes; let her live that life, for it is better justice and more terrible. I can love those that gave me such a thought."

And the lepers answered:

"Throw her among us, and make her one of us. Never shall lady have known a worse end. And look," they said, "at our rags and our abominations. She has had pleasure in rich stuffs and furs, jewels and walls of marble, honour, good wines and joy, but when she sees your lepers always, King, and only them for ever, their couches and their huts, then indeed she will know the wrong she has done, and bitterly desire even that great flame of thorns."

And as the King heard them, he stood a long time without moving; then he ran to the Queen and seized her by the hand, and she cried:

"Burn me! rather burn me!"

But the King gave her up, and Ivan took her, and the hundred lepers pressed around, and to hear her cries all the crowd rose in pity. But Ivan had an evil gladness, and as he went he dragged her out of the borough bounds, with his hideous company.

Now they took that road where Tristan lay in hiding, and Gorvenal said to him:

"Son, here is your friend. Will you do naught?"

Then Tristan mounted the horse and spurred it out of the bush, and cried:

"Ivan, you have been at the Queen's side a moment, and too long. Now leave her if you would live."

But Ivan threw his cloak away and shouted:

"Your clubs, comrades, and your staves! Crutches in the air—for a fight is on!"

Then it was fine to see the lepers throwing their capes aside, and stirring their sick legs, and brandishing their crutches, some threatening: groaning all; but to strike them Tristan was too noble. There are singers who sing that Tristan killed Ivan, but it is a lie. Too much a knight was he to kill such things. Gorvenal indeed, snatching up an oak sapling, crashed it on Ivan's head till his blood ran down to his misshapen feet. Then Tristan took the Queen.

Henceforth near him she felt no further evil. He cut the cords that bound her arms so straightly, and he left the plain so that they plunged into the wood of Morois; and there in the thick wood Tristan was as sure as in a castle keep.

And as the sun fell they halted all three at the foot of a little hill: fear had wearied the Queen, and she leant her head upon his body and slept.

But in the morning, Gorvenal stole from a wood man his bow and two good arrows plumed and barbed, and gave them to Tristan, the great archer, and he shot him a fawn and killed it. Then Gorvenal gathered dry twigs, struck flint, and lit a great fire to cook the venison. And Tristan cut him branches and made a hut and garnished it with leaves. And Iseult slept upon the thick leaves there.

So, in the depths of the wild wood began for the lovers that savage life which yet they loved very soon.

PART THE SECOND

THE WOOD OF MOROIS

They wandered in the depths of the wild wood, restless and in haste like beasts that are hunted, nor did they often dare to return by night to the shelter of yesterday. They ate but the flesh of wild animals. Their faces sank and grew white, their clothes ragged; for the briars tore them. They loved each other and they did not know that they suffered.

One day, as they were wandering in these high woods that had never yet been felled or ordered, they came upon the hermitage of Ogrin.

The old man limped in the sunlight under a light growth of maples near his chapel: he leant upon his crutch, and cried:

"Lord Tristan, hear the great oath which the Cornish men have sworn. The King has published a ban in every parish: Whosoever may seize you shall receive a hundred marks of gold for his guerdon, and all the barons have sworn to give you up alive or dead. Do penance, Tristan! God pardons the sinner who turns to repentance."

"And of what should I repent, Ogrin, my lord? Or of what crime? You that sit in judgment upon us here, do you know what cup it was we drank upon the high sea? That good, great draught inebriates us both. I would rather beg my life long and live of roots and herbs with Iseult than, lacking her, be king of a wide kingdom."

"God aid you, Lord Tristan; for you have lost both this world and the next. A man that is traitor to his lord is worthy to be torn by horses and burnt upon the faggot, and wherever his ashes fall no grass shall grow and all tillage is waste, and the trees and the green things die. Lord Tristan, give back the Queen to the man who espoused her lawfully according to the laws of Rome."

"He gave her to his lepers. From these lepers I myself conquered her with my own hand; and henceforth she is altogether mine. She cannot pass from me nor I from her."

Ogrin sat down; but at his feet Iseult, her head upon the knees of that man of God, wept silently. The hermit told her and re-told her the words of his holy book, but still while she wept she shook her head, and refused the faith he offered.

"Ah me," said Ogrin then, "what comfort can one give the dead? Do penance, Tristan, for a man who lives in sin without repenting is a man quite dead."

"Oh no," said Tristan, "I live and I do no penance. We will go back into the high wood which comforts and wards us all round about. Come with me, Iseult, my friend."

Iseult rose up; they held each other's hands. They passed into the high grass and the underwood: the trees hid them with their branches. They disappeared beyond the leaves.

The summer passed and the winter came: the two lovers lived, all hidden in the hollow of a rock, and on the frozen earth the cold crisped their couch with dead leaves. In the strength of their love neither one nor the other felt these mortal things. But when the open skies had come back with the springtime, they built a hut of green branches under the great trees. Tristan had known, ever since his childhood, that art by which a man may sing the song of birds in the woods, and at his fancy, he would call as call the thrush, the blackbird and the nightingale, and all winged things; and sometimes in reply very many birds would come on to the branches of his hut and sing their song full-throated in the new light.

The lovers had ceased to wander through the forest, for none of the barons ran the risk of their pursuit knowing well that Tristan would have hanged them to the branches of a tree. One day, however, one of the four traitors, Guenelon, whom God blast! drawn by the heat of the hunt, dared enter the Morois. And that morning, on the forest edge in a ravine, Gorvenal, having unsaddled his horse, had let him graze on the new grass, while far off in their hut Tristan held the Queen, and they slept. Then suddenly Gorvenal heard the cry of the pack; the hounds pursued a deer, which fell into that ravine. And far on the heath the hunter showed — and Gorvenal knew him for the man whom his master hated above all. Alone, with bloody spurs, and striking his horse's mane, he galloped on; but Gorvenal watched him from ambush: he came fast, he would return more slowly. He passed and Gorvenal leapt from his ambush and seized the rein and, suddenly, remembering all the wrong that man had done, hewed him to death and carried off his head in his hands. And when the hunters found the body, as they followed, they thought Tristan came after and they fled in fear of death, and thereafter no man hunted in that wood. And far off, in the hut upon their couch of leaves, slept Tristan and the Queen.

There came Gorvenal, noiseless, the dead man's head in his hands that he might lift his master's heart at his awakening. He hung it by its hair outside the hut, and the leaves garlanded it about. Tristan woke and saw it, half hidden in the leaves, and staring at him as he gazed, and he became afraid. But Gorvenal said: "Fear not, he is dead. I killed him with this sword."

Then Tristan was glad, and henceforward from that day no one dared enter the wild wood, for terror guarded it and the lovers were lords of it all: and then it was that Tristan fashioned his bow "Failnaught" which struck home always, man or beast, whatever it aimed at.

My lords, upon a summer day, when mowing is, a little after Whitsuntide, as the birds sang dawn Tristan left his hut and girt his sword on him, and took his bow "Failnaught" and went off to hunt in the wood; but before evening, great evil was to fall on him, for no lovers ever loved so much or paid their love so dear.

When Tristan came back, broken by the heat, the Queen said

"Friend, where have you been?"

"Hunting a hart," he said, "that wearied me. I would lie down and sleep."

So she lay down, and he, and between them Tristan put his naked sword, and on the Queen's finger was that ring of gold with emeralds set therein, which Mark had given her on her bridal day; but her hand was so wasted that the ring hardly held. And no wind blew, and no leaves stirred, but through a crevice in the branches a sunbeam fell upon the face of Iseult and it shone white like ice. Now a woodman found in the wood a place where the leaves were crushed, where the lovers had halted and slept, and he followed their track and found the hut, and saw them sleeping and fled off, fearing the terrible awakening of that lord. He fled to Tintagel, and going up the stairs of the palace, found the King as he held his pleas in hall amid the vassals assembled.

"Friend," said the King, "what came you hither to seek in haste and breathless, like a huntsman that has followed the dogs afoot? Have you some wrong to right, or has any man driven you?"

But the woodman took him aside and said low down:

"I have seen the Queen and Tristan, and I feared and fled."

"Where saw you them?"

"In a hut in Morois, they slept side by side. Come swiftly and take your vengeance."

"Go," said the King, "and await me at the forest edge where the red cross stands, and tell no man what you have seen. You shall have gold and silver at your will."

The King had saddled his horse and girt his sword and left the city alone, and as he rode alone he minded him of the night when he

46

had seen Tristan under the great pine-tree, and Iseult with her clear face, and he thought:

"If I find them I will avenge this awful wrong."

At the foot of the red cross he came to the woodman and said:

"Go first, and lead me straight and quickly."

The dark shade of the great trees wrapt them round, and as the King followed the spy he felt his sword, and trusted it for the great blows it had struck of old; and surely had Tristan wakened, one of the two had stayed there dead. Then the woodman said:

"King, we are near."

He held the stirrup, and tied the rein to a green apple-tree, and saw in a sunlit glade the hut with its flowers and leaves. Then the King cast his cloak with its fine buckle of gold and drew his sword from its sheath and said again in his heart that they or he should die. And he signed to the woodman to be gone.

He came alone into the hut, sword bare, and watched them as they lay: but he saw that they were apart, and he wondered because between them was the naked blade.

Then he said to himself: "My God, I may not kill them. For all the time they have lived together in this wood, these two lovers, yet is the sword here between them, and throughout Christendom men know that sign. Therefore I will not slay, for that would be treason and wrong, but I will do so that when they wake they may know that I found them here, asleep, and spared them and that God had pity on them both."

And still the sunbeam fell upon the white face of Iseult, and the King took his ermined gloves and put them up against the crevice whence it shone.

Then in her sleep a vision came to Iseult. She seemed to be in a great wood and two lions near her fought for her, and she gave a cry and woke, and the gloves fell upon her breast; and at the cry Tristan woke, and made to seize his sword, and saw by the golden hilt that it was the King's. And the Queen saw on her finger the King's ring, and she cried:

"O, my lord, the King has found us here!"

And Tristan said:

"He has taken my sword; he was alone, but he will return, and will burn us before the people. Let us fly."

So by great marches with Gorvenal alone they fled towards Wales.

OGRIN THE HERMIT

After three days it happened that Tristan, in following a wounded deer far out into the wood, was caught by night-fall, and took to thinking thus under the dark wood alone:

"It was not fear that moved the King ... he had my sword and I slept ... and had he wished to slay, why did he leave me his own blade? ... O, my father, my father, I know you now. There was pardon in your heart, and tenderness and pity ... yet how was that, for who could forgive in this matter without shame? ... It was not pardon it was understanding; the faggot and the chantry leap and the leper ambush have shown him God upon our side. Also I think he remembered the boy who long ago harped at his feet, and my land of Lyonesse which I left for him; the Morholt's spear and blood shed in his honour. He remembered how I made no avowal, but claimed a trial at arms, and the high nature of his heart has made him understand what men around him cannot; never can he know of the spell, yet he doubts and hopes and knows I have told no lie, and would have me prove my cause. O, but to win at arms by God's aid for him, and to enter his peace and to put on mail for him again ... but then he must take her back, and I must yield her ... it would have been much better had he killed me in my sleep. For till now I was hunted and I could hate and forget; he had thrown Iseult to the lepers, she was no more his, but mine; and now by his compassion he has wakened my heart and regained the Queen. For Queen she was at his side, but in this wood she lives a slave, and I waste her youth; and for rooms all hung with silk she has this savage place, and a hut for her splendid walls, and I am the cause that she treads this ugly road. So now I cry to God the Lord, who is King of the world, and beg Him to give me strength to yield back Iseult to King Mark; for she is indeed his wife, wed according to the laws of Rome before all the Barony of his land."

And as he thought thus, he leant upon his bow, and all through the night considered his sorrow.

49

Within the hollow of thorns that was their resting-place Iseult the Fair awaited Tristan's return. The golden ring that King Mark had slipped there glistened on her finger in the moonlight, and she thought:

"He that put on this ring is not the man who threw me to his lepers in his wrath; he is rather that compassionate lord who, from the day I touched his shore, received me and protected. And he loved Tristan once, but I came, and see what I have done! He should have lived in the King's palace; he should have ridden through King's and baron's fees, finding adventure; but through me he has forgotten his knighthood, and is hunted and exiled from the court, leading a random life. ..."

Just then she heard the feet of Tristan coming over the dead leaves and twigs. She came to meet him, as was her wont, to relieve him of his arms, and she took from him his bow, "Failnaught," and his arrows, and she unbuckled his sword-straps. And, "Friend," said he, "it is the King's sword. It should have slain, but it spared us."

Iseult took the sword, and kissed the hilt of gold, and Tristan saw her weeping.

"Friend," said he, "if I could make my peace with the King; if he would allow me to sustain in arms that neither by act nor word have I loved you with a wrongful love, any knight from the Marshes of Ely right away to Dureaume that would gainsay me, would find me armed in the ring. Then if the King would keep you and drive me out I would cross to the Lowlands or to Brittany with Gorvenal alone. But wherever I went and always, Queen, I should be yours; nor would I have spoken thus, Iseult, but for the wretchedness you bear so long for my sake in this desert land."

"Tristan," she said, "there is the hermit Ogrin. Let us return to him, and cry mercy to the King of Heaven."

They wakened Gorvenal; Iseult mounted the steed, and Tristan led it by the bridle, and all night long they went for the last time through the woods of their love, and they did not speak a word. By morning they came to the Hermitage, where Ogrin read at the threshold, and seeing them, called them tenderly:

"Friends," he cried, "see how Love drives you still to further wretchedness. Will you not do penance at last for your madness?"

"Lord Ogrin," said Tristan, "hear us. Help us to offer peace to the King, and I will yield him the Queen, and will myself go far away into Brittany or the Lowlands, and if some day the King suffer me, I will return and serve as I should."

And at the hermit's feet Iseult said in her turn:

"Nor will I live longer so, for though I will not say one word of penance for my love, which is there and remains forever, yet from now on I will be separate from him." Then the hermit wept and praised God and cried: "High King, I praise Thy Name, for that Thou hast let me live so long as to give aid to these!"

And he gave them wise counsel, and took ink, and wrote a little writ offering the King what Tristan said. That night Tristan took the road. Once more he saw the marble well and the tall pine-tree, and he came beneath the window where the King slept, and called him gently, and Mark awoke and whispered: "Who are you that call me in the night at such an hour?"

"Lord, I am Tristan: I bring you a writ, and lay it here."

Then the King cried: "Nephew! nephew! for God's sake wait awhile," but Tristan had fled and joined his squire, and mounted rapidly. Gorvenal said to him: "O, Tristan, you are mad to have come. Fly hard with me by the nearest road."

So they came back to the Hermitage, and there they found Ogrin at prayer, but Iseult weeping silently.

THE FORD

Mark had awakened his chaplain and had given him the writ to read; the chaplain broke the seal, saluted in Tristan's name, and then, when he had cunningly made out the written words, told him what Tristan offered; and Mark heard without saying a word, but his heart was glad, for he still loved the Queen.

He summoned by name the choicest of his baronage, and when they were all assembled they were silent and the King spoke:

"My lords, here is a writ, just sent me. I am your King, and you my lieges. Hear what is offered me, and then counsel me, for you owe me counsel."

The chaplain rose, unfolded the writ, and said, upstanding

"My lords, it is Tristan that first sends love and homage to the King and all his Barony, and he adds, 'O King, when I slew the dragon and conquered the King of Ireland's daughter it was to me they gave her. I was to ward her at will and I yielded her to you. Yet hardly had you wed her when felons made you accept their lies, and in your anger, fair uncle, my lord, you would have had us burnt without trial. But God took compassion on us; we prayed him and he saved the Queen, as justice was: and me also—though I leapt from a high rock, I was saved by the power of God. And since then what have I done blameworthy? The Queen was thrown to the lepers; I came to her succour and bore her away. Could I have done less for a woman, who all but died innocent through me? I fled through the woods. Nor could I have come down into the vale and yielded her, for there was a ban to take us dead or alive. But now, as then, I am ready, my lord, to sustain in arms against all comers that never had the Queen for me, nor I for her a love dishonourable to you. Publish the lists, and if I cannot prove my right in arms, burn me before your men. But if I conquer and you take back Iseult, no baron of yours will serve you as will I; and if you will not have me, I will offer myself to the King of Galloway, or to him of the

53

Lowlands, and you will hear of me never again. Take counsel, King, for if you will make no terms I will take back Iseult to Ireland, and she shall be Queen in her own land.'"

When the barons of Cornwall heard how Tristan offered battle, they said to the King:

"Sire, take back the Queen. They were madmen that belied her to you. But as for Tristan, let him go and war it in Galloway, or in the Lowlands. Bid him bring back Iseult on such a day and that soon.

Then the King called thrice clearly:

"Will any man rise in accusation against Tristan?"

And as none replied, he said to his chaplain:

"Write me a writ in haste. You have heard what you shall write. Iseult has suffered enough in her youth. And let the writ be hung upon the arm of the red cross before evening. Write speedily."

Towards midnight Tristan crossed the Heath of Sand, and found the writ, and bore it sealed to Ogrin; and the hermit read the letter; "How Mark consented by the counsel of his barons to take back Iseult, but not to keep Tristan for his liege. Rather let him cross the sea, when, on the third day hence, at the Ford of Chances, he had given back the Queen into King Mark's hands." Then Tristan said to the Queen:

"O, my God! I must lose you, friend! But it must be, since I can thus spare you what you suffer for my sake. But when we part for ever I will give you a pledge of mine to keep, and from whatever unknown land I reach I will send some messenger, and he will bring back word of you, and at your call I will come from far away."

Iseult said, sighing:

"Tristan, leave me your dog, Toothold, and every time I see him I will remember you, and will be less sad. And, friend, I have here a ring of green jasper. Take it for the love of me, and put it on your finger; then if anyone come saying he is from you, I will not trust him at all till he show me this ring, but once I have seen it, there is no power or royal ban that can prevent me from doing what you bid—wisdom or folly."

"Friend," he said, "here give I you Toothold."

"Friend," she replied, "take you this ring in reward."

And they kissed each other on the lips.

Now Ogrin, having left the lovers in the Hermitage, hobbled upon his crutch to the place called The Mount, and he bought ermine there and fur and cloth of silk and purple and scarlet, and a palfrey harnessed in gold that went softly, and the folk laughed to see him spending upon these the small moneys he had amassed so long; but the old man put the rich stuffs upon the palfrey and came back to Iseult.

And "Queen," said he, "take these gifts of mine that you may seem the finer on the day when you come to the Ford."

Meanwhile the King had had cried through Cornwall the news that on the third day he would make his peace with the Queen at the Ford, and knights and ladies came in a crowd to the gathering, for all loved the Queen and would see her, save the three felons that yet survived.

On the day chosen for the meeting, the field shone far with the rich tents of the barons, and suddenly Tristan and Iseult came out at the forest's edge, and caught sight of King Mark far off among his Barony:

"Friend," said Tristan, "there is the King, your lord—his knights and his men; they are coming towards us, and very soon we may not speak to each other again. By the God of Power I conjure you, if ever I send you a word, do you my bidding."

"Friend," said Iseult, "on the day that I see the ring, nor tower, nor wall, nor stronghold will let me from doing the will of my friend."

"Why then," he said, "Iseult, may God reward you."

Their horses went abreast and he drew her towards him with his arm.

"Friend," said Iseult, "hear my last prayer: you will leave this land, but wait some days; hide till you know how the King may treat me, whether in wrath or kindness, for I am afraid. Friend, Orri the woodman will entertain you hidden. Go you by night to the abandoned cellar that you know and I will send Perinis there to say if anyone misuse me."

"Friend, none would dare. I will stay hidden with Orri, and if any misuse you let him fear me as the Enemy himself."

Now the two troops were near and they saluted, and the King rode a bow-shot before his men and with him Dinas of Lidan; and when the barons had come up, Tristan, holding Iseult's palfrey by the bridle, bowed to the King and said:

"O King, I yield you here Iseult the Fair, and I summon you, before the men of your land, that I may defend myself in your court, for I have had no judgment. Let me have trial at arms, and if I am conquered, burn me, but if I conquer, keep me by you, or, if you will not, I will be off to some far country."

But no one took up Tristan's wager, and the King, taking Iseult's palfrey by the bridle, gave it to Dinas, and went apart to take counsel.

Dinas, in his joy, gave all honour and courtesy to the Queen, but when the felons saw her so fair and honoured as of old, they were stirred and rode to the King, and said:

"King, hear our counsel. That the Queen was slandered we admit, but if she and Tristan re-enter your court together, rumour will revive again. Rather let Tristan go apart awhile. Doubtless some day you may recall him."

And so Mark did, and ordered Tristan by his barons to go off without delay.

Then Tristan came near the Queen for his farewell, and as they looked at one another the Queen in shame of that assembly blushed, but the King pitied her, and spoke his nephew thus for the first time:

"You cannot leave in these rags; take then from my treasury gold and silver and white fur and grey, as much as you will."

"King," said Tristan, "neither a penny nor a link of mail. I will go as I can, and serve with high heart the mighty King in the Lowlands."

And he turned rein and went down towards the sea, but Iseult followed him with her eyes, and so long as he could yet be seen a long way off she did not turn.

Now at the news of the peace, men, women, and children, great and small, ran out of the town in a crowd to meet Iseult, and while they mourned Tristan's exile they rejoiced at the Queen's return.

And to the noise of bells, and over pavings strewn with branches, the King and his counts and princes made her escort, and the gates of the palace were thrown open that rich and poor might enter and eat and drink at will.

And Mark freed a hundred of his slaves, and armed a score of squires that day with hauberk and with sword.

But Tristan that night hid with Orri, as the Queen had counselled him.

THE ORDEAL BY IRON

Denoalen, Andret, and Gondoin held themselves safe; Tristan was far over sea, far away in service of a distant king, and they beyond his power. Therefore, during a hunt one day, as the King rode apart in a glade where the pack would pass, and hearkening to the hounds, they all three rode towards him, and said:

"O King, we have somewhat to say. Once you condemned the Queen without judgment, and that was wrong; now you acquit her without judgment, and that is wrong. She is not quit by trial, and the barons of your land blame you both. Counsel her, then, to claim the ordeal in God's judgment, for since she is innocent, she may swear on the relics of the saints and hot iron will not hurt her. For so custom runs, and in this easy way are doubts dissolved."

But Mark answered:

"God strike you, my Cornish lords, how you hunt my shame! For you have I exiled my nephew, and now what would you now? Would you have me drive the Queen to Ireland too? What novel plaints have you to plead? Did not Tristan offer you battle in this matter? He offered battle to clear the Queen forever: he offered and you heard him all. Where then were your lances and your shields?"

"Sire," they said, "we have counselled you loyal counsel as lieges and to your honour; henceforward we hold our peace. Put aside your anger and give us your safe-guard."

But Mark stood up in the stirrup and cried:

"Out of my land, and out of my peace, all of you! Tristan I exiled for you, and now go you in turn, out of my land!"

But they answered:

"Sire, it is well. Our keeps are strong and fenced, and stand on rocks not easy for men to climb."

And they rode off without a salutation.

But the King (not tarrying for huntsman or for hound but straight away) spurred his horse to Tintagel; and as he sprang up the stairs the Queen heard the jangle of his spurs upon the stones.

She rose to meet him and took his sword as she was wont, and bowed before him, as it was also her wont to do; but Mark raised her, holding her hands; and when Iseult looked up she saw his noble face in just that wrath she had seen before the faggot fire.

She thought that Tristan was found, and her heart grew cold, and without a word she fell at the King's feet.

He took her in his arms and kissed her gently till she could speak again, and then he said:

"Friend, friend, what evil tries you?"

"Sire, I am afraid, for I have seen your anger.

"Yes, I was angered at the hunt."

"My lord, should one take so deeply the mischances of a game?"

Mark smiled and said:

"No, friend; no chance of hunting vexed me, but those three felons whom you know; and I have driven them forth from my land."

"Sire, what did they say, or dare to say of me?"

"What matter? I have driven them forth."

"Sire, all living have this right: to say the word they have conceived. And I would ask a question, but from whom shall I learn save from you? I am alone in a foreign land, and have no one else to defend me."

"They would have it that you should quit yourself by solemn oath and by the ordeal of iron, saying 'that God was a true judge, and that as the Queen was innocent, she herself should seek such judgment as would clear her for ever.' This was their clamour and their demand incessantly. But let us leave it. I tell you, I have driven them forth."

Iseult trembled, but looking straight at the King, she said:

"Sire, call them back; I will clear myself by oath. But I bargain this: that on the appointed day you call King Arthur and Lord Gawain, Girflet, Kay the Seneschal, and a hundred of his knights to ride to the Sandy Heath where your land marches with his, and a river flows between; for I will not swear before your barons alone, lest they should demand some new thing, and lest there should be no end to my trials. But if my warrantors, King Arthur and his knights, be there, the barons will not dare dispute the judgment."

But as the heralds rode to Carduel, Iseult sent to Tristan secretly her squire Perinis: and he ran through the underwood, avoiding paths, till he found the hut of Orri, the woodman, where Tristan for many days had awaited news. Perinis told him all: the ordeal, the place, and the time, and added:

"My lord, the Queen would have you on that day and place come dressed as a pilgrim, so that none may know you—unarmed, so that none may challenge —to the Sandy Heath. She must cross the river to the place appointed. Beyond it, where Arthur and his hundred knights will stand, be you also; for my lady fears the judgment, but she trusts in God."

Then Tristan answered:

"Go back, friend Perinis, return you to the Queen, and say that I will do her bidding."

And you must know that as Perinis went back to Tintagel he caught sight of that same woodman who had betrayed the lovers before, and the woodman, as he found him, had just dug a pitfall for wolves and for wild boars, and covered it with leafy branches to hide it, and as Perinis came near the woodman fled, but Perinis drove him, and caught him, and broke his staff and his head together, and pushed his body into the pitfall with his feet.

On the appointed day King Mark and Iseult, and the barons of Cornwall, stood by the river; and the knights of Arthur and all their host were arrayed beyond.

And just before them, sitting on the shore, was a poor pilgrim, wrapped in cloak and hood, who held his wooden platter and begged alms.

Now as the Cornish boats came to the shoal of the further bank, Iseult said to the knights:

"My lords, how shall I land without befouling my clothes in the river-mud? Fetch me a ferryman."

And one of the knights hailed the pilgrim, and said:

"Friend, truss your coat, and try the water; carry you the Queen to shore, unless you fear the burden."

But as he took the Queen in his arms she whispered to him:

"Friend."

And then she whispered to him, lower still

"Stumble you upon the sand."

And as he touched shore, he stumbled, holding the Queen in his arms; and the squires and boatmen with their oars and boat-hooks drove the poor pilgrim away.

But the Queen said:

"Let him be; some great travail and journey has weakened him."

And she threw to the pilgrim a little clasp of gold.

Before the tent of King Arthur was spread a rich Nicean cloth upon the grass, and the holy relics were set on it, taken out of their covers and their shrines.

And round the holy relics on the sward stood a guard more than a king's guard, for Lord Gawain, Girflet, and Kay the Seneschal kept ward over them.

The Queen having prayed God, took off the jewels from her neck and hands, and gave them to the beggars around; she took off her purple mantle, and her overdress, and her shoes with their precious stones, and gave them also to the poor that loved her.

She kept upon her only the sleeveless tunic, and then with arms and feet quite bare she came between the two kings, and all around the barons watched her in silence, and some wept, for near the holy relics was a brazier burning.

And trembling a little she stretched her right hand towards the bones and said: "Kings of Logres and of Cornwall; my lords Gawain, and Kay, and Girflet, and all of you that are my warrantors, by these holy things and all the holy things of earth, I swear that no man has held me in his arms saving King Mark, my lord, and that poor pilgrim. King Mark, will that oath stand?"

"Yes, Queen," he said, "and God see to it.

"Amen," said Iseult, and then she went near the brazier, pale and stumbling, and all were silent. The iron was red, but she thrust her bare arms among the coals and seized it, and bearing it took nine steps.

Then, as she cast it from her, she stretched her arms out in a cross, with the palms of her hands wide open, and all men saw them fresh and clean and cold. Seeing that great sight the kings and the barons and the people stood for a moment silent, then they stirred together and they praised God loudly all around.

PART THE THIRD

THE LITTLE FAIRY BELL

When Tristan had come back to Orri's hut, and had loosened his heavy pilgrim's cape, he saw clearly in his heart that it was time to keep his oath to King Mark and to fly the land.

Three days yet he tarried, because he could not drag himself away from that earth, but on the fourth day he thanked the woodman, and said to Gorvenal:

"Master, the hour is come."

And he went into Wales, into the land of the great Duke Gilain, who was young, powerful, and frank in spirit, and welcomed him nobly as a God-sent guest.

And he did everything to give him honour and joy; but he found that neither adventure, nor feast could soothe what Tristan suffered.

One day, as he sat by the young Duke's side, his spirit weighed upon him, so that not knowing it he groaned, and the Duke, to soothe him, ordered into his private room a fairy thing, which pleased his eyes when he was sad and relieved his own heart; it was a dog, and the varlets brought it in to him, and they put it upon a table there. Now this dog was a fairy dog, and came from the Duke of Avalon; for a fairy had given it him as a love-gift, and no one can well describe its kind or beauty. And it bore at its neck, hung to a little chain of gold, a little bell; and that tinkled so gaily, and so clear and so soft, that as Tristan heard it, he was soothed, and his anguish melted away, and he forgot all that he had suffered for the Queen; for such was the virtue of the bell and such its property: that whosoever heard it, he lost all pain. And as Tristan stroked the little fairy thing, the dog that took away his sorrow, he saw how delicate it was and fine, and how it had soft hair like samite, and he thought how good a gift it would make for the Queen. But he dared not ask for it right out since he knew that the Duke loved this dog beyond everything in the world, and would yield it to no prayers, nor to wealth, nor to wile; so one day Tristan having made a plan in his mind said this:

"Lord, what would you give to the man who could rid your land of the hairy giant Urgan, that levies such a toll?"

"Truly, the victor might choose what he would, but none will dare."

Then said Tristan:

"Those are strange words, for good comes to no land save by risk and daring, and not for all the gold of Milan would I renounce my desire to find him in his wood and bring him down."

Then Tristan went out to find Urgan in his lair, and they fought hard and long, till courage conquered strength, and Tristan, having cut off the giant's hand, bore it back to the Duke.

And "Sire," said he, "since I may choose a reward according to your word, give me the little fairy dog. It was for that I conquered Urgan, and your promise stands."

"Friend," said the Duke, "take it, then, but in taking it you take away also all my joy."

Then Tristan took the little fairy dog and gave it in ward to a Welsh harper, who was cunning and who bore it to Cornwall till he came to Tintagel, and having come there put it secretly into Brangien's hands, and the Queen was so pleased that she gave ten marks of gold to the harper, but she put it about that the Queen of Ireland, her mother, had sent the beast. And she had a goldsmith work a little kennel for him, all jewelled, and incrusted with gold and enamel inlaid; and wherever she went she carried the dog with her in memory of her friend, and as she watched it sadness and anguish and regrets melted out of her heart.

At first she did not guess the marvel, but thought her consolation was because the gift was Tristan's, till one day she found that it was fairy, and that it was the little bell that charmed her soul; then she thought: "What have I to do with comfort since he is sorrowing? He could have kept it too and have forgotten his sorrow; but with high courtesy he sent it to me to give me his joy and to take up his pain again. Friend, while you suffer, so long will I suffer also."

And she took the magic bell and shook it just a little, and then by the open window she threw it into the sea.

ISEULT OF THE WHITE HANDS

Apart the lovers could neither live nor die, for it was life and death together; and Tristan fled his sorrow through seas and islands and many lands.

He fled his sorrow still by seas and islands, till at last he came back to his land of Lyonesse, and there Rohalt, the keeper of faith, welcomed him with happy tears and called him son. But he could not live in the peace of his own land, and he turned again and rode through kingdoms and through baronies, seeking adventure. From the Lyonesse to the Lowlands, from the Lowlands on to the Germanies; through the Germanies and into Spain. And many lords he served, and many deeds did, but for two years no news came to him out of Cornwall, nor friend, nor messenger. Then he thought that Iseult had forgotten.

Now it happened one day that, riding with Gorvenal alone, he came into the land of Brittany. They rode through a wasted plain of ruined walls and empty hamlets and burnt fields everywhere, and the earth deserted of men; and Tristan thought:

"I am weary, and my deeds profit me nothing; my lady is far off and I shall never see her again. Or why for two years has she made no sign, or why has she sent no messenger to find me as I wandered? But in Tintagel Mark honours her and she gives him joy, and that little fairy bell has done a thorough work; for little she remembers or cares for the joys and the mourning of old, little for me, as I wander in this desert place. I, too, will forget."

On the third day, at the hour of noon, Tristan and Gorvenal came near a hill where an old chantry stood and close by a hermitage also; and Tristan asked what wasted land that was, and the hermit answered:

"Lord, it is Breton land which Duke Hod holds, and once it was rich in pasture and ploughland, but Count Riol of Nantes has wasted it.

For you must know that this Count Riol was the Duke's vassal. And the Duke has a daughter, fair among all King's daughters, and Count Riol would have taken her to wife; but her father refused her to a vassal, and Count Riol would have carried her away by force. Many men have died in that quarrel."

And Tristan asked:

"Can the Duke wage his war?"

And the hermit answered:

"Hardly, my lord; yet his last keep of Carhaix holds out still, for the walls are strong, and strong is the heart of the Duke's son Kaherdin, a very good knight and bold; but the enemy surrounds them on every side and starves them. Very hardly do they hold their castle."

Then Tristan asked:

"How far is this keep of Carhaix?"

"Sir," said the hermit, "it is but two miles further on this way."

Then Tristan and Gorvenal lay down, for it was evening.

In the morning, when they had slept, and when the hermit had chanted, and had shared his black bread with them, Tristan thanked him and rode hard to Carhaix. And as he halted beneath the fast high walls, he saw a little company of men behind the battlements, and he asked if the Duke were there with his son Kaherdin. Now Hod was among them; and when he cried "yes," Tristan called up to him and said:

"I am that Tristan, King of Lyonesse, and Mark of Cornwall is my uncle. I have heard that your vassals do you a wrong, and I have come to offer you my arms.

"Alas, lord Tristan, go you your way alone and God reward you, for here within we have no more food; no wheat, or meat, or any stores but only lentils and a little oats remaining."

70

But Tristan said

"For two years I dwelt in a forest, eating nothing save roots and herbs; yet I found it a good life, so open you the door."

They welcomed him with honour, and Kaherdin showed him the wall and the dungeon keep with all their devices, and from the battlements he showed the plain where far away gleamed the tents of Duke Riol. And when they were down in the castle again he said to Tristan:

"Friend, let us go to the hall where my mother and sister sit."

So, holding each other's hands, they came into the women's room, where the mother and the daughter sat together weaving gold upon English cloth and singing a weaving song. They sang of Doette the fair who sits alone beneath the white-thorn, and round about her blows the wind. She waits for Doon, her friend, but he tarries long and does not come. This was the song they sang. And Tristan bowed to them, and they to him. Then Kaherdin, showing the work his mother did, said:

"See, friend Tristan, what a work-woman is here, and how marvellously she adorns stoles and chasubles for the poor minsters, and how my sister's hands run thread of gold upon this cloth. Of right, good sister, are you called, 'Iseult of the White Hands.'"

But Tristan, hearing her name, smiled and looked at her more gently.

And on the morrow, Tristan, Kaherdin, and twelve young knights left the castle and rode to a pinewood near the enemy's tents. And sprang from ambush and captured a waggon of Count Riol's food; and from that day, by escapade and ruse they would carry tents and convoys and kill off men, nor ever come back without some booty; so that Tristan and Kaherdin began to be brothers in arms, and kept faith and tenderness, as history tells. And as they came back from these rides, talking chivalry together, often did Kaherdin praise to his comrade his sister, Iseult of the White Hands, for her simplicity and beauty.

One day, as the dawn broke, a sentinel ran from the tower through the halls crying:

"Lords, you have slept too long; rise, for an assault is on."

And knights and burgesses armed, and ran to the walls, and saw helmets shining on the plain, and pennons streaming crimson, like flames, and all the host of Riol in its array. Then the Duke and Kaherdin deployed their horsemen before the gates, and from a bow-length off they stooped, and spurred and charged, and they put their lances down together and the arrows fell on them like April rain.

Now Tristan had armed himself among the last of those the sentinel had roused, and he laced his shoes of steel, and put on his mail, and his spurs of gold, his hauberk, and his helm over the gorget, and he mounted and spurred, with shield on breast, crying:

"Carhaix!"

And as he came, he saw Duke Riol charging, rein free, at Kaherdin, but Tristan came in between. So they met, Tristan and Duke Riol. And at the shock, Tristan's lance shivered, but Riol's lance struck Tristan's horse just where the breast-piece runs, and laid it on the field.

But Tristan, standing, drew his sword, his burnished sword, and said:

"Coward! Here is death ready for the man that strikes the horse before the rider."

But Riol answered:

"I think you have lied, my lord!"

And he charged him.

And as he passed, Tristan let fall his sword so heavily upon his helm that he carried away the crest and the nasal, but the sword slipped on the mailed shoulder, and glanced on the horse, and killed it, so that of force Duke Riol must slip the stirrup and leap and feel the ground. Then Riol too was on his feet, and they both fought hard in their broken mail, their 'scutcheons torn and their helmets loosened and lashing with their dented swords, till Tristan struck Riol just where the helmet buckles, and it yielded and the blow was struck so hard that the baron fell on hands and knees; but when he had risen again, Tristan struck him down once more with a blow that split the helm, and it split the headpiece too, and touched the skull; then Riol cried mercy and begged his life, and Tristan took his sword.

So he promised to enter Duke Hoël's keep and to swear homage again, and to restore what he had wasted; and by his order the battle ceased, and his host went off discomfited.

Now when the victors were returned Kaherdin said to his father:

"Sire, keep you Tristan. There is no better knight, and your land has need of such courage."

So when the Duke had taken counsel with his barons, he said to Tristan

"Friend, I owe you my land, but I shall be quit with you if you will take my daughter, Iseult of the White Hands, who comes of kings and of queens, and of dukes before them in blood."

And Tristan answered:

"I will take her, Sire."

So the day was fixed, and the Duke came with his friends and Tristan with his, and before all, at the gate of the minster, Tristan wed Iseult of the White Hands, according to the Church's law.

But that same night, as Tristan's valets undressed him, it happened that in drawing his arm from the sleeve they drew off and let fall from his finger the ring of green jasper, the ring of Iseult the Fair. It sounded on the stones, and Tristan looked and saw it. Then his heart awoke and he knew that he had done wrong. For he remembered the day when Iseult the Fair had given him the ring. It was in that forest where, for his sake, she had led the hard life with him, and that night he saw again the hut in the wood of Morois, and he was bitter with himself that ever he had accused her of treason; for now it was he that had betrayed, and he was bitter with himself also in pity for this new wife and her simplicity and beauty. See how these two Iseults had met him in an evil hour, and to both had he broken faith!

Now Iseult of the White Hands said to him, hearing him sigh:

"Dear lord, have I hurt you in anything? Will you not speak me a single word?"

But Tristan answered: "Friend, do not be angry with me; for once in another land I fought a foul dragon and was near to death, and I thought of the Mother of God, and I made a vow to Her that, should I ever wed, I would spend the first holy nights of my wedding in prayer and in silence."

"Why," said Iseult, "that was a good vow."

And Tristan watched through the night.

THE MADNESS OF TRISTAN

Within her room at Tintagel, Iseult the Fair sighed for the sake of Tristan, and named him, her desire, of whom for two years she had had no word, whether he lived or no.

Within her room at Tintagel Iseult the Fair sat singing a song she had made. She sang of Guron taken and killed for his love, and how by guile the Count gave Guron's heart to her to eat, and of her woe. The Queen sang softly, catching the harp's tone; her hands were cunning and her song good; she sang low down and softly.

Then came in Kariado, a rich count from a far-off island, that had fared to Tintagel to offer the Queen his service, and had spoken of love to her, though she disdained his folly. He found Iseult as she sang, and laughed to her:

"Lady, how sad a song! as sad as the Osprey's; do they not say he sings for death? and your song means that to me; I die for you."

And Iseult said: "So let it be and may it mean so; for never come you here but to stir in me anger or mourning. Ever were you the screech owl or the Osprey that boded ill when you spoke of Tristan; what news bear you now?"

And Kariado answered:

"You are angered, I know not why, but who heeds your words? Let the Osprey bode me death; here is the evil news the screech owl brings. Lady Iseult, Tristan, your friend is lost to you. He has wed in a far land. So seek you other where, for he mocks your love. He has wed in great pomp Iseult of the White Hands, the King of Brittany's daughter."

And Kariado went off in anger, but Iseult bowed her head and broke into tears.

Now far from Iseult, Tristan languished, till on a day he must needs see her again. Far from her, death came surely; and he had rather die at once than day by day. And he desired some death, but that the Queen might know it was in finding her; then would death come easily.

So he left Carhaix secretly, telling no man, neither his kindred nor even Kaherdin, his brother in arms. He went in rags afoot (for no one marks the beggar on the high road) till he came to the shore of the sea.

He found in a haven a great ship ready, the sail was up and the anchor-chain short at the bow.

"God save you, my lords," he said, "and send you a good journey. To what land sail you now?"

"To Tintagel," they said.

Then he cried out:

"Oh, my lords! take me with you thither!"

And he went aboard, and a fair wind filled the sail, and she ran five days and nights for Cornwall, till, on the sixth day, they dropped anchor in Tintagel Haven. The castle stood above, fenced all around. There was but the one armed gate, and two knights watched it night and day. So Tristan went ashore and sat upon the beach, and a man told him that Mark was there and had just held his court.

"But where," said he, "is Iseult, the Queen, and her fair maid, Brangien?"

"In Tintagel too," said the other, "and I saw them lately; the Queen sad, as she always is."

At the hearing of the name, Tristan suffered, and he thought that neither by guile nor courage could he see that friend, for Mark would kill him.

And he thought, "Let him kill me and let me die for her, since every day I die. But you, Iseult, even if you knew me here, would you not drive me out?" And he thought, "I will try guile. I will seem mad, but with a madness that shall be great wisdom. And many shall think me a fool that have less wit than I."

Just then a fisherman passed in a rough cloak and cape, and Tristan seeing him, took him aside, and said:

"Friend, will you not change clothes?"

And as the fisherman found it a very good bargain, he said in answer:

"Yes, friend, gladly."

And he changed and ran off at once for fear of losing his gain. Then Tristan shaved his wonderful hair; he shaved it close to his head and left a cross all bald, and he rubbed his face with magic herbs distilled in his own country, and it changed in colour and skin so that none could know him, and he made him a club from a young tree torn from a hedge-row and hung it to his neck, and went bare-foot towards the castle.

The porter made sure that he had to do with a fool and said:

"Good morrow, fool, where have you been this long while?"

And he answered:

"At the Abbot of St. Michael's wedding, and he wed an abbess, large and veiled. And from the Alps to Mount St. Michael how they came, the priests and abbots, monks and regulars, all dancing on the green with croziers and with staves under the high trees' shade. But I left them all to come hither, for I serve at the King's board to-day."

Then the porter said:

"Come in, lord fool; the Hairy Urgan's son, I know, and like your father."

And when he was within the courts the serving men ran after him and cried:

"The fool! the fool!"

But he made play with them though they cast stones and struck him as they laughed, and in the midst of laughter and their cries, as the rout followed him, he came to that hall where, at the Queen's side, King Mark sat under his canopy.

And as he neared the door with his club at his neck, the King said:

"Here is a merry fellow, let him in."

And they brought him in, his club at his neck. And the King said:

"Friend, well come; what seek you here?"

"Iseult," said he, "whom I love so well; I bring my sister with me, Brunehild, the beautiful. Come, take her, you are weary of the Queen. Take you my sister and give me here Iseult, and I will hold her and serve you for her love."

The King said laughing:

"Fool, if I gave you the Queen, where would you take her, pray?"

"Oh! very high," he said, "between the clouds and heaven, into a fair chamber glazed. The beams of the sun shine through it, yet the winds do not trouble it at all. There would I bear the Queen into that crystal chamber of mine all compact of roses and the morning."

The King and his barons laughed and said:

"Here is a good fool at no loss for words."

But the fool as he sat at their feet gazed at Iseult most fixedly.

"Friend," said King Mark, "what warrant have you that the Queen would heed so foul a fool as you?"

"O! Sire," he answered gravely, "many deeds have I done for her, and my madness is from her alone."

"What is your name?" they said, and laughed.

"Tristan," said he, "that loved the Queen so well, and still till death will love her."

But at the name the Queen angered and weakened together, and said: "Get hence for an evil fool!"

But the fool, marking her anger, went on:

"Queen Iseult, do you mind the day, when, poisoned by the Morholt's spear, I took my harp to sea and fell upon your shore? Your mother healed me with strange drugs. Have you no memory, Queen?"

But Iseult answered:

"Out, fool, out! Your folly and you have passed the bounds!"

But the fool, still playing, pushed the barons out, crying:

"Out! madmen, out! Leave me to counsel with Iseult, since I come here for the love of her!"

And as the King laughed, Iseult blushed and said:

"King, drive me forth this fool!"

But the fool still laughed and cried:

"Queen, do you mind you of the dragon I slew in your land? I hid its tongue in my hose, and, burnt of its venom, I fell by the roadside. Ah! what a knight was I then, and it was you that succoured me."

Iseult replied:

"Silence! You wrong all knighthood by your words, for you are a fool from birth. Cursed be the seamen that brought you hither; rather should they have cast you into the sea!"

"Queen Iseult," he still said on, "do you mind you of your haste when you would have slain me with my own sword? And of the Hair of Gold? And of how I stood up to the seneschal?"

"Silence!" she said, "you drunkard. You were drunk last night, and so you dreamt these dreams."

"Drunk, and still so am I," said he, "but of such a draught that never can the influence fade. Queen Iseult, do you mind you of that hot and open day on the high seas? We thirsted and we drank together from the same cup, and since that day have I been drunk with an awful wine."

When the Queen heard these words which she alone could understand, she rose and would have gone.

But the King held her by her ermine cloak, and she sat down again.

And as the King had his fill of the fool he called for his falcons and went to hunt; and Iseult said to him:

"Sire, I am weak and sad; let me be go rest in my room; I am tired of these follies."

And she went to her room in thought and sat upon her bed and mourned, calling herself a slave and saying:

"Why was I born? Brangien, dear sister, life is so hard to me that death were better! There is a fool without, shaven criss-cross, and come in an evil hour, and he is warlock, for he knows in every part myself and my whole life; he knows what you and I and Tristan only know."

Then Brangien said: "It may be Tristan."

But—"No," said the Queen, "for he was the first of knights, but this fool is foul and made awry. Curse me his hour and the ship that brought him hither."

"My lady!" said Brangien, "soothe you. You curse over much these days. May be he comes from Tristan?"

"I cannot tell. I know him not. But go find him, friend, and see if you know him."

So Brangien went to the hall where the fool still sat alone. Tristan knew her and let fall his club and said:

"Brangien, dear Brangien, before God! have pity on me!"

"Foul fool," she answered, "what devil taught you my name?"

"Lady," he said, "I have known it long. By my head, that once was fair, if I am mad the blame is yours, for it was yours to watch over the wine we drank on the high seas. The cup was of silver and I held it to Iseult and she drank. Do you remember, lady?"

"No," she said, and as she trembled and left he called out: "Pity me!"

He followed and saw Iseult. He stretched out his arms, but in her shame, sweating agony she drew back, and Tristan angered and said:

"I have lived too long, for I have seen the day that Iseult will nothing of me. Iseult, how hard love dies! Iseult, a welling water that floods and runs large is a mighty thing; on the day that it fails it is nothing; so love that turns."

But she said

"Brother, I look at you and doubt and tremble, and I know you not for Tristan."

"Queen Iseult, I am Tristan indeed that do love you; mind you for the last time of the dwarf, and of the flower, and of the blood I

81

shed in my leap. Oh! and of that ring I took in kisses and in tears on the day we parted. I have kept that jasper ring and asked it counsel."

Then Iseult knew Tristan for what he was, and she said:

"Heart, you should have broken of sorrow not to have known the man who has suffered so much for you. Pardon, my master and my friend."

And her eyes darkened and she fell; but when the light returned she was held by him who kissed her eyes and her face.

So passed they three full days. But, on the third, two maids that watched them told the traitor Andret, and he put spies well-armed before the women's rooms. And when Tristan would enter they cried:

"Back, fool!"

But he brandished his club laughing, and said:

"What! May I not kiss the Queen who loves me and awaits me now?"

And they feared him for a mad fool, and he passed in through the door.

Then, being with the Queen for the last time, he held her in his arms and said:

"Friend, I must fly, for they are wondering. I must fly, and perhaps shall never see you more. My death is near, and far from you my death will come of desire."

"Oh friend," she said, "fold your arms round me close and strain me so that our hearts may break and our souls go free at last. Take me to that happy place of which you told me long ago. The fields whence none return, but where great singers sing their songs for ever. Take me now."

"I will take you to the Happy Palace of the living, Queen! The time is near. We have drunk all joy and sorrow. The time is near. When it is finished, if I call you, will you come, my friend?"

"Friend," said she, "call me and you know that I shall come."

"Friend," said he, "God send you His reward."

As he went out the spies would have held him; but he laughed aloud, and flourished his club, and cried:

"Peace, gentlemen, I go and will not stay. My lady sends me to prepare that shining house I vowed her, of crystal, and of rose shot through with morning."

And as they cursed and drave him, the fool went leaping on his way.

THE DEATH OF TRISTAN

When he was come back to Brittany, to Carhaix, it happened that Tristan, riding to the aid of Kaherdin his brother in arms, fell into ambush and was wounded by a poisoned spear; and many doctors came, but none could cure him of the ill. And Tristan weakened and paled, and his bones showed.

Then he knew that his life was going, and that he must die, and he had a desire to see once more Iseult the Fair, but he could not seek her, for the sea would have killed him in his weakness, and how could Iseult come to him? And sad, and suffering the poison, he awaited death.

He called Kaherdin secretly to tell him his pain, for they loved each other with a loyal love; and as he would have no one in the room save Kaherdin, nor even in the neighbouring rooms, Iseult of the White Hands began to wonder. She was afraid and wished to hear, and she came back and listened at the wall by Tristan's bed; and as she listened one of her maids kept watch for her.

Now, within, Tristan had gathered up his strength, and had half risen, leaning against the wall, and Kaherdin wept beside him. They wept their good comradeship, broken so soon, and their friendship: then Tristan told Kaherdin of his love for that other Iseult, and of the sorrow of his life.

"Fair friend and gentle," said Tristan, "I am in a foreign land where I have neither friend nor cousin, save you; and you alone in this place have given me comfort. My life is going, and I wish to see once more Iseult the Fair. Ah, did I but know of a messenger who would go to her! For now I know that she will come to me. Kaherdin, my brother in arms, I beg it of your friendship; try this thing for me, and if you carry my word, I will become your liege, and I will cherish you beyond all other men."

85

And as Kaherdin saw Tristan broken down, his heart reproached him and he said:

"Fair comrade, do not weep; I will do what you desire, even if it were risk of death I would do it for you. Nor no distress nor anguish will let me from doing it according to my power. Give me the word you send, and I will make ready."

And Tristan answered:

"Thank you, friend; this is my prayer: take this ring, it is a sign between her and me; and when you come to her land pass yourself at court for a merchant, and show her silk and stuffs, but make so that she sees the ring, for then she will find some ruse by which to speak to you in secret. Then tell her that my heart salutes her; tell her that she alone can bring me comfort; tell her that if she does not come I shall die. Tell her to remember our past time, and our great sorrows, and all the joy there was in our loyal and tender love. And tell her to remember that draught we drank together on the high seas. For we drank our death together. Tell her to remember the oath I swore to serve a single love, for I have kept that oath."

But behind the wall, Iseult of the White Hands heard all these things; and Tristan continued:

"Hasten, my friend, and come back quickly, or you will not see me again. Take forty days for your term, but come back with Iseult the Fair. And tell your sister nothing, or tell her that you seek some doctor. Take my fine ship, and two sails with you, one white, one black. And as you return, if you bring Iseult, hoist the white sail; but if you bring her not, the black. Now I have nothing more to say, but God guide you and bring you back safe."

With the first fair wind Kaherdin took the open, weighed anchor and hoisted sail, and ran with a light air and broke the seas. They bore rich merchandise with them, dyed silks of rare colours, enamel of Touraine and wines of Poitou, for by this ruse Kaherdin thought to reach Iseult. Eight days and nights they ran full sail to Cornwall.

Now a woman's wrath is a fearful thing, and all men fear it, for according to her love, so will her vengeance be; and their love and their hate come quickly, but their hate lives longer than their love; and they will make play with love, but not with hate. So Iseult of the White Hands, who had heard every word, and who had so loved Tristan, waited her vengeance upon what she loved most in the world. But she hid it all; and when the doors were open again she came to Tristan's bed and served him with food as a lover should, and spoke him gently and kissed him on the lips, and asked him if Kaherdin would soon return with one to cure him … but all day long she thought upon her vengeance.

And Kaherdin sailed and sailed till he dropped anchor in the haven of Tintagel. He landed and took with him a cloth of rare dye and a cup well chiselled and worked, and made a present of them to King Mark, and courteously begged of him his peace and safeguard that he might traffick in his land; and the King gave him his peace before all the men of his palace.

Then Kaherdin offered the Queen a buckle of fine gold; and "Queen," said he, "the gold is good."

Then taking from his finger Tristan's ring, he put it side by side with the jewel and said:

"See, O Queen, the gold of the buckle is the finer gold; yet that ring also has its worth."

When Iseult saw what ring that was, her heart trembled and her colour changed, and fearing what might next be said she drew Kaherdin apart near a window, as if to see and bargain the better; and Kaherdin said to her, low down:

"Lady, Tristan is wounded of a poisoned spear and is about to die. He sends you word that you alone can bring him comfort, and recalls to you the great sorrows that you bore together. Keep you the ring—it is yours."

But Iseult answered, weakening:

"Friend, I will follow you; get ready your ship to-morrow at dawn."

And on the morrow at dawn they raised anchor, stepped mast, and hoisted sail, and happily the barque left land.

But at Carhaix Tristan lay and longed for Iseult's coming. Nothing now filled him any more, and if he lived it was only as awaiting her; and day by day he sent watchers to the shore to see if some ship came, and to learn the colour of her sail. There was no other thing left in his heart.

He had himself carried to the cliff of the Penmarks, where it overlooks the sea, and all the daylight long he gazed far off over the water.

Hear now a tale most sad and pitiful to all who love. Already was Iseult near; already the cliff of the Penmarks showed far away, and the ship ran heartily, when a storm wind rose on a sudden and grew, and struck the sail, and turned the ship all round about, and the sailors bore away and sore against their will they ran before the wind. The wind raged and big seas ran, and the air grew thick with darkness, and the ocean itself turned dark, and the rain drove in gusts. The yard snapped, and the sheet; they struck their sail, and ran with wind and water. In an evil hour they had forgotten to haul their pinnace aboard; it leapt in their wake, and a great sea broke it away.

Then Iseult cried out: "God does not will that I should live to see him, my love, once—even one time more. God wills my drowning in this sea. O, Tristan, had I spoken to you but once again, it is little I should have cared for a death come afterwards. But now, my love, I cannot come to you; for God so wills it, and that is the core of my grief."

And thus the Queen complained so long as the storm endured; but after five days it died down. Kaherdin hoisted the sail, the white sail, right up to the very masthead with great joy; the white sail, that Tristan might know its colour from afar: and already Kaherdin saw Britanny far off like a cloud. Hardly were these things seen and done when a calm came, and the sea lay even and untroubled. The sail bellied no longer, and the sailors held the ship now up, now down, the tide, beating backwards and forwards in vain. They saw the shore afar off, but the storm had carried their boat away and they could not land. On the third night Iseult dreamt this dream: that she held in her lap a boar's head which befouled her skirts with blood; then she knew that she would never see her lover again alive.

Tristan was now too weak to keep his watch from the cliff of the Penmarks, and for many long days, within walls, far from the shore, he had mourned for Iseult because she did not come. Dolorous and alone, he mourned and sighed in restlessness: he was near death from desire.

At last the wind freshened and the white sail showed. Then it was that Iseult of the White Hands took her vengeance.

She came to where Tristan lay, and she said:

"Friend, Kaherdin is here. I have seen his ship upon the sea. She comes up hardly—yet I know her; may he bring that which shall heal thee, friend."

And Tristan trembled and said:

"Beautiful friend, you are sure that the ship is his indeed? Then tell me what is the manner of the sail?"

"I saw it plain and well. They have shaken it out and hoisted it very high, for they have little wind. For its colour, why, it is black."

And Tristan turned him to the wall, and said:

89

"I cannot keep this life of mine any longer." He said three times: "Iseult, my friend." And in saying it the fourth time, he died.

Then throughout the house, the knights and the comrades of Tristan wept out loud, and they took him from his bed and laid him on a rich cloth, and they covered his body with a shroud. But at sea the wind had risen; it struck the sail fair and full and drove the ship to shore, and Iseult the Fair set foot upon the land. She heard loud mourning in the streets, and the tolling of bells in the minsters and the chapel towers; she asked the people the meaning of the knell and of their tears. An old man said to her:

"Lady, we suffer a great grief. Tristan, that was so loyal and so right, is dead. He was open to the poor; he ministered to the suffering. It is the chief evil that has ever fallen on this land."

But Iseult, hearing them, could not answer them a word. She went up to the palace, following the way, and her cloak was random and wild. The Bretons marvelled as she went; nor had they ever seen woman of such a beauty, and they said:

"Who is she, or whence does she come?"

Near Tristan, Iseult of the White Hands crouched, maddened at the evil she had done, and calling and lamenting over the dead man. The other Iseult came in and said to her:

"Lady, rise and let me come by him; I have more right to mourn him than have you—believe me. I loved him more."

And when she had turned to the east and prayed God, she moved the body a little and lay down by the dead man, beside her friend. She kissed his mouth and his face, and clasped him closely; and so gave up her soul, and died beside him of grief for her lover.

When King Mark heard of the death of these lovers, he crossed the sea and came into Brittany; and he had two coffins hewn, for Tristan and Iseult, one of chalcedony for Iseult, and one of beryl for Tristan. And he took their beloved bodies away with him upon his ship to Tintagel, and by a chantry to the left and right of the apse he had their tombs built round. But in one night there sprang from the tomb of Tristan a green and leafy briar, strong in its branches and in the scent of its flowers. It climbed the chantry and fell to root again by Iseult's tomb. Thrice did the peasants cut it down, but thrice it grew again as flowered and as strong. They told the marvel to King Mark, and he forbade them to cut the briar any more.

The good singers of old time, Beroul and Thomas of Built, Gilbert and Gottfried told this tale for lovers and none other, and, by my pen, they beg you for your prayers. They greet those who are cast down, and those in heart, those troubled and those filled with desire. May all herein find strength against inconstancy and despite and loss and pain and all the bitterness of loving.

Made in the USA
Middletown, DE
03 February 2015